Orly Castel-Bloom

AN EGYPTIAN NOVEL

Translated from the Hebrew by Todd Hasak-Lowy

DALKEY ARCHIVE PRESS

Originally published in Hebrew by Hakibbutz Hameuchad/Siman Kriah as *Ha-Roman Ha-Mitzri* in 2015.

First Dalkey Archive edition, 2017.

Library of Congress Cataloging-in-Publication Data
Names: Castel-Bloom, Orly, 1960- author. | Hasak-Lowy, Todd, 1969- translator.
Title: An Egyptian novel / by Orly Castel-Bloom ; translation by Todd Hasak-Lowy.
Other titles: Roman ha-Mitsri. English
Description: Victoria, TX : Dalkey Archive Press, [2017]
Identifiers: LCCN 2017006134 | ISBN 9781943150229 (pbk. : alk. paper)
Classification: LCC PJ5054.C37 R6613 2015 | DDC 892.43/6--dc23
LC record available at https://lccn.loc.gov/2017006134

Published by arrangement with the Institute for the Translation of Hebrew Literature.

www.dalkeyarchive.com
Victoria, TX / McLean, IL / Dublin

Dalkey Archive Press publications are, in part, made possible through the support of the University of Houston-Victoria and its programs in creative writing, publishing, and translation.

Printed on permanent/durable acid-free paper

An Egyptian Novel

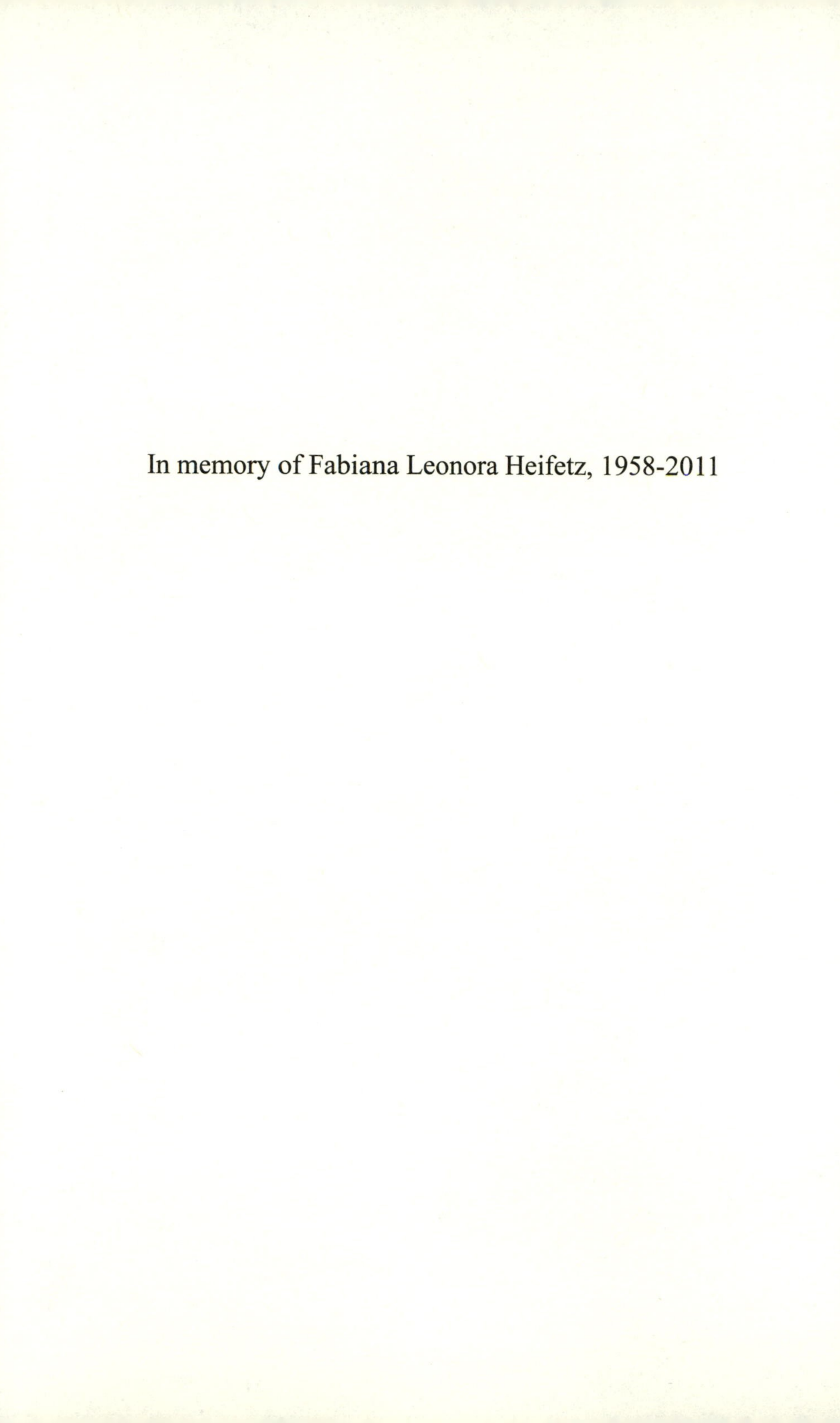

In memory of Fabiana Leonora Heifetz, 1958-2011

Chapter One
Wedding in Karkur

He said he'd come on a tractor through the fields, Vivienne repeated while looking at herself in the mirror of the bank's bathroom and combing her hair. She wasn't pleased. Her hair wasn't working out right. Nevertheless today is her wedding day. True she has no bridal gown, and everything will take place at top speed in the house of Karkur's rabbi, but a wedding! Breaking a glass, making vows. From now on she won't be different from the others, from the rest of those kicked out of the Egyptian *garin*, some of whom are already pregnant, and a few already have a child who runs—and not behind them anymore! She won't be different than her sisters either! The two of them were already married at the magnificent "Gates of Heaven" synagogue in Cairo. What grief she felt when she couldn't make it to their weddings. She was already in Israel by then, on the kibbutz.

Vivienne was twenty-six years old, and lagged behind everyone, and this was my oh my.

Charlie was the youngest of five brothers who were born one after the other while still in Egypt, during the first half of the previous century, to Flore and David Casteel, after three daughters who died one after the other because there wasn't good enough medicine for them back then. One of them passed from typhus at age seven, a second from smallpox at age ten, and a third died at the age of eleven, from the bursting of an appendix. Their mother Flore died of sorrow at the age of fifty, and she was buried in Cairo, not in Gaza as Vivienne had first thought.

Vivienne's mother was also called Flore, but Vivienne's family had already been in Egypt for centuries, for too many centuries, perhaps even millennia, because apparently, as her mother Flore had told her, they belonged to that clan, to that one and only household they don't talk about in the history of the Jewish people—those who during the great exodus rejected Moses and remained in Egypt as slaves. Only centuries later were they freed and became wild hunters, and when Jews reached Egypt after the expulsion from Spain, they hurried to join them, because they sensed in some vague, mystical way an ancient affinity.

Charlie was a thin, very quiet man, stuck in his own world. He didn't recover from the deaths of his three sisters, and in particular from the influence their death had on his mother, who until her dying day held Charlie, her eighth child, born to elderly parents, close to her.

Vivienne discerned the presence of the past within Charlie by his reticence, and the frequency with which he blinked his eyes, and the massive amount of cigarettes he smoked. She believed thanks to this wound actually that Charlie, as a family man, devoted to one family, would be satisfied and would seek out a steady income that went to only one family, and wouldn't scream loudly like her two brothers, whose screams during her childhood could be heard throughout Cairo's Heliopolis quarter, to the point that Vivienne and her two sisters, Cecile and Solange, were embarrassed to walk in the street.

And Vivienne also wished that he wouldn't beat or betray her. But let's suppose he beat her—this she could still absorb, even though she couldn't promise that she wouldn't take painful revenge—but that he'd cheat on her? That she'd have partners in him, and that they'd know she's being cheated on? She would be unable to bear the loss this shame would bring to her.

She'd never be able to forget the drama that her mother made for her father, once the cat was out of the bag and it became clear that his income was being divided into two, and not even equally. True that what her father did right under everyone's nose for perhaps twenty years was never mentioned, but almost everyone knew. With Vivienne nothing even resembling this will happen. She'll keep seven eyes open, day and night. Okay, one affair at the most, two at the most, but a fifteen, even twenty, yearlong story, and with children? All her radars are tuned to find out, according to signals that she and her sisters sat and talked about at Rich Café, where they wondered how it could be that their mother didn't notice, and analyzed it all in depth, and assumed that she was stuck caring for the firstborn.

Other than her sisters who were already married, Charlie's brother, Vita, was already married to Adele, who didn't like the yellow part of the hard-boiled egg, and told everyone in the Egyptian *garin*—their cohort on the kibbutz—that she's half-Ashkenazi. At the dining hall they gave her two eggs, because they knew she ate only the white part. She would give the yolks to her husband, Vivienne's future brother-in-law. Vivienne didn't understand the connection between the fact that she was half-Ashkenazi and that she didn't like the yellow part of the egg, but in the dining hall Adele would always mention these facts together.

At six she needs to be at the rabbi's house. True he came from Iran, but the ceremony won't be Persian but nonsectarian instead. It didn't matter to Vivienne which melodies there would be, the point was to get it over with already and be married like everyone else. Charlie told her the melodies didn't matter to him either. He's bringing a few liras that he'll secretly give to the rabbi, so the rabbi will do his job and send them on their way without driving them crazy. Charlie's too anti-religious for her tastes. And he's also too Communist. Put every last bit of himself into the matter, "*Hashomer Hatsair*," the Young Guard, "*Hashomer Hatsair*."

Vivienne figured that she ought to leave Tel Aviv by three at the latest. She'd put on makeup in Karkur, in the mirror of the rabbi's bathroom. She'd take all her makeup with her in a bag. She doesn't have much. Who would photograph her? Definitely not she herself.

She returned to her spot in the bank and said to her supervisor:

"I have to leave early today, Mr. Konforti." A Bulgarian name.

"Why?" Mr. Konforti asked.

"I have a wedding."

"Everyone has a wedding sometimes, what, so everyone's going to start leaving early every time? We'll call it a day whenever?" Mr. Konforti said.

"No, no. I'm getting married myself." All her life she was timid, but inside her the eternal flame burned.

"You?" Mr. Konforti was dumbfounded. "Today?"

"Yes. In Karkur. In order to be there on time I need to leave early. I'm traveling by Egged bus."

"What kind of wedding is this?"

"A wedding with a rabbi. Real fast. Tomorrow I'm here."

"And where's the groom?"

"On a kibbutz. Serving there."

"And you're in Tel Aviv?"

"Until the wedding," she laughed to herself, and then kicked away her thoughts, so as not to rummage around in that disturbing place. She had no idea what would be after the wedding. They hadn't talked about it. She had her wishes, but they hadn't agreed on a thing. She left Kibbutz Ein-Shemer together with the entire Egyptian *garin*, whereas he was to finish four years of service on the kibbutz, which were equivalent to compulsory military service. Kibbutz life enchanted him all on its own. Especially the crops and the kitchen.

Strange, thought Vivienne, a man who only two or three years ago hopped around proud and independent, with a fez on his head, in the streets of Cairo during the demonstrations by the Egyptian left, and shouted epithets against King Farouk, in whom Vivienne saw no faults but rather brilliance instead—even if his people in one day expelled her family from the respected neighborhood to a more ordinary neighborhood—a person like this, it's as if he's completely spineless, he becomes a Zionist and suddenly falls in love with kibbutz life, which lacks all logic in the opinion of Vivienne, whose entire life has waited for the moment when she'd have something of her own that she wouldn't have to share with sisters and "members."

The members of the *garin* came from different neighborhoods in Cairo, and *Hashomer Hatsair* combined them all and brought them out of Egypt to the kibbutz, and from the kibbutz expelled them on a bus to Hadera, as will still be told. Supposedly it should have been clear that after the wedding Charlie would join his brother Vita, and the rest of the group that had already made a place for itself in the big city Tel Aviv, or in the new city Holon, whose neighborhoods were being built.

"Leave now," the Bulgarian supervisor, who had mobilized his entire being for her benefit, said to her at one in the afternoon. "So you'll have time to prepare yourself for your wedding. To put on a wedding gown."

"I don't have a wedding gown . . ." Vivienne laughed, "these are the clothes . . ."

She tensed up and showed him the two-piece gray-white suit, very chic, in her bag, with the highly fashionable heeled shoes. Very coquettish.

"Congratulations," Konforti said slowly, and suddenly, as if he wanted to wake her, as if he wanted to wake up the entire world, called out, "*I don't understand why didn't you take the day off?*"

"No need," Vivienne said and lowered her head bashfully.

"Leave at one-fifteen. When's your Egged to Karkur? Where does it leave from?"

"Every two hours, on the hours divisible by two, from the Central Bus Station."

"Catch the one at two," the supervisor said after looking at his watch with concern. "When exactly is the wedding?"

"At six, at the rabbi's . . ."

His face fell.

"So what will you do all that time?"

"Don't worry."

She left at one-thirty in order to have time to stop at the hairdresser's, who for two payments, one this month and one next month, gave her a very beautiful hairdo that would hold until Karkur. She was happy, because there was no solution to her hair. Charlie didn't have hair like that, and in light of his genetics and that of his four brothers, most of whom she'd met, she very much hoped that the children born to them would take their hair from him, it was especially desirable that this would happen if they have daughters, because then, when they're older, they wouldn't need to waste money on hairdressers. In general Vivienne hoped that the children would take a lot from him, and this was despite the fact that she barely knew him. Her oldest brother had caused her self-confidence to deteriorate to this extent.

In terms of beauty, if they had daughters, it was of course desirable that they'd also take from her middle sister, and if there were sons—from her tall oldest brother, with the handsome face, who in their youth wanted them to bring everything on a tray to his bed, and since she refused to serve him, would hit her at night using the excuse that he was dreaming it. Every other night he would sleepwalk from his and his brothers' room to the girls' room, attack her and give her a beating. The whole house would wake up from her screams. And since everything happened in the midst of a very deep sleep, it was twice as hard to get him off her. Deep emotional wounds her brother brought forth from those dreams.

Vivienne wore a jacket over her suit, because it was an especially cold day. She intended to give the jacket, immediately after the wedding, to her sister who had settled in Jerusalem with her husband. She hadn't even dreamt of inviting her to the wedding in Karkur. This was her beautiful sister, whose mustached husband was a levelheaded person, who never let a wrong word leave his mouth, and who would always support his arguments with evidence from different dictionaries he had within reach, or by means of a penetrating, frightening glance.

At the rabbi's house, at a quarter to six, they didn't open the door for her, because no one was home. Vivienne sat down carefully on the stone railing by the entrance, and with the help of a small mirror, which she took out from her bag, she fixed the makeup they gave her on the house at the hairdresser. She had time to smoke a cigarette. The rabbi returned home at five to six and brought her into the living room. Charlie arrived a bit late, driving a tractor from which two girls, whom Vivienne didn't know, hung, one on each side. He wore a white shirt and work pants, and was sparkling clean and giving off the high quality aftershave he always had on, the one that he equipped himself with in France, on their way to Israel, his small stock of it kept hidden in one of the kibbutz's sheds. He had a heavy bundle of keys, on which were keys to all the sheds that he hid from every guard. This time he didn't bring the massive bundle with him. For certain he left it in trustworthy hands with a remorseful heart.

"Arrives to the wedding on a tractor through the fields . . ." Vivienne said to herself. More people arrived, but via the regular route, and perhaps someone from among the five people who came to the wedding from the center of Israel were even among those who paved the road along which they now travelled to Vivienne and Charlie's wedding. All in all a dozen men and women arrived, and the men, in order to complete their *minyan* for the needs of the seven wedding blessings, went off to hunt for volunteers from among the passersby in the street.

During the ceremony there were a lot of jokes tossed about.

Someone said something and everyone laughed. Vivienne herself smiled the entire ceremony, but was determined not to show her teeth, so that no one would see that they weren't straightened as was once proper. Charlie was scatterbrained. His head moved in every direction like a student not paying attention in class, and even the rabbi commented to him that he was disturbing his own wedding ceremony and that he should settle down. The kiss was rushed. When the people were about to disperse Charlie said to Vivienne:

"You'll return to Tel Aviv with Vita and Adele, and I'll return to the kibbutz with Miriam and Fula."

He spoke in French. "I have two more weeks to finish at the kibbutz. Stupid for me to travel every day back and forth, back and forth. I'll come in another two weeks."

"Of course," Vivienne agreed. "Very stupid to travel every day back and forth, back and forth." She expected that at the least he'd return with her to Tel Aviv that evening, and they'd go out to celebrate, and he'd stay to spend the night, and catch the first or second bus to the kibbutz. She wouldn't be able to take him to the second, because she didn't say anything about it at work, but to the first she definitely could.

Chapter Two
Adele's Suitcase

ADELE DIDN'T EVEN have the tiniest fraction of Zionism in her. Zionism, Communism, Socialism—jokes, that's what they were in her eyes, jokes that should be sprayed and removed, in order to leave everything spic-and-span for the true things in life: love, quiet, beauty, sufficient amounts of healthy food (never too much), beautiful clothes, and if needed, as became clear over the years, doctors too.

Adele didn't really want to go to Israel. Yes she devoutly ran the activities of the Jabes chapter of *Hashomer Hatsair* in Cairo, but she did this solely because of Vita the counselor. Her long-term plan was to settle in France, near her half-sister Beatrice, and pursue higher education in chemistry at the Sorbonne.

Only through the power of her love for the handsome and noble-minded Vita—proponent of equality and brotherhood, diligent and serious activist in Cairo's chapters of *Hashomer Hatsair*, who longed to reach Israel, and who in exchange returned to her a true and loyal love until his dying day—did she alter her plans: she arrived in Israel and from there began setting her life in motion.

Already as a teen she noticed that this was an extraordinary guy, rare and not another one like him, for whom it was worth it to alter all plans and fill oneself up with any idealism, the main thing was to conquer his heart.

Adele's father had been banished from his Sephardic family, because he married a German Ashkenazi woman. He died when Adele was two months old, and here she now has for herself, Adele does, a pure Sephardic man *par excellence.* Oedipus had a ball with her. Adele knew more details about Vita's heritage than Vivienne knew about Charlie's. Indeed, this was the very same heritage, only Charlie never ever spoke about it, those roots didn't interest him in the slightest, whereas Vita talked about them over and over.

During the expulsion of the Jews from Spain, after great upheaval and loss, seven brothers got on a ship, and afterwards got on another ship, and it's reasonable to assume on another one as well, until they reached the port in Gaza, and in this city they settled. Vita's forebears fought the Sabbateans, and Rabbi Shmuel Casteel was the first to build a synagogue in Gaza, after they got rid of them.

Even though Adele was now hearing, from Vita her love, about Sabbateans for the first time in her life, she immediately understood that these were historical facts. As a future chemist, with a lucid, scientific soul, she valued facts and data wherever they were. And in general, a false word never left her mouth, and if by chance she had no choice, and had to come up with a lie—she would immediately change the subject.

The romantic chronicles of the seven brothers, passing from ship to ship after the expulsion from Spain, until they reached the shore of Gaza, combined with Vita's thick head of hair and dark brown skin, skin that nevertheless grew reddish when he tanned, not brown or black—a sign of pure pigmentation in the family—and especially in combination with his highly devoted soul, they subdued Adele. She knew she had a trump card for the rest of her life.

His confident, persuasive speech, and the complete protection he gave her from the rest of the world, caused her to forget the Sorbonne and Paris (but not chemistry). If one must get down under the cow's belly and milk it—why she'd lie there on her back, on the straw, on some clean padded pillow she brought with her, on which were embroidered her mother's flowers; she'd lie among all the Romanian immigrants she couldn't stand, and pull on the cows' udders with gloveless hands, because with gloves she couldn't get a thing out of them. Only with exposed fingers, despite all the rules of hygiene bequeathed to her by her German mother.

"No that's not it," Adele ans wered the question of the rabbi who had come from Pardes-Hannah to the cabin of the Egyptian *garin* at Kibbutz Ein-Shemer in order to marry her to her Vita, hers and how, and at this same opportunity marry another six couples (among whom not every one was, respectively, every one else's, but most of them were), and he married all of them with one ring that was passed from couple to couple.

The rabbi repeated the question. Adele had already learned Hebrew in the kibbutz's *ulpan*, and she understood quite well that he was asking her if she was Ashkenazic or Sephardic.

"Not either," she said again. "I know that my father died when I was two months old."

The rabbi therefore interrogated her: her mother's maiden name, her father's full name—and immediately found that Adele is Sephardic from her father's side, and German-Ashkenazic from her mother's side.

A week after the wedding Vita too was suddenly moved to milking, and as someone who had seen the young female milkers from the Romanian *garin*, Adele grew rather worried. Feminine beauty was determined for her according to degree of paleness, and the Romanians were paler than her, and hence beauties, and nothing in life was new to them. These were young women aged sixteen or seventeen, and Vita was supposed to wake them in the morning, if they didn't get up on their own, the prima donnas, and if he didn't succeed in waking them up by knocking on the door of their quarters, he was authorized to open the door and enter the room and gently shake them.

What is this whole kibbutz thing about? She didn't know. A married man enters the rooms of young women who aren't missing a thing and touches them so they'll get up to milk cows?

After a milking shift there was a shepherding shift waiting for Vita, and only then, when Vita was with the flock, could Adele allow herself to grab some sleep.

The burden on her shoulders was too great in this new place, but Vita loved this life, and according to what she saw on the horizon, there was no way out of the kibbutz. She had to wear the ugly clothes she got from their shed, and to see Nina or Haya'le in the dress that she herself bought in France, they spent a few weeks there at a "training" farm in La Roche, Bourgogne between Paris and Dijon, before arriving at this remote corner in Israel. The dress complimented Nina very much, it seemed to hang off of Haya'le: Adele has no idea how this Haya'le pigs out nonstop and remains thin. Perhaps because she also blabbers nonstop.

Her dress reached Israel in her suitcase. And when she had to, when she was already at the kibbutz, share her possessions with all the members, Adele fought for her suitcase, but not for any of its contents. An intense discussion concerning the suitcase was held in the cabin of the Egyptian *garin*. Tall Lizette, who was very extreme when it came to the division of property, ran this meeting. Adele fought for her suitcase as if it were gold and there was no socialism in the world, and Tall Lizette responded with warfare of insane, Stalinistic fervor.

This was a beautiful, rigid suitcase, covered in plaid, which opened into a small closet with multiple cubicles as well as small drawers with transparent handles resembling diamonds, the likes of which had never been seen before. It had great sentimental value: she and her mother packed the suitcase together before she traveled to the training farm in La Roche.

She refused to comprehend what Lizette wanted with her suitcase. Hadn't they already arrived in the kibbutz; indeed they were supposed to remain here fifty, sixty years, no? So why did she, Lizette, care if she, Adele, kept the suitcase with her as a keepsake from her mother? Indeed she wouldn't be traveling anywhere in the next fifty years either!

A day later Lizette organized a for-or-against vote, and she had arguments in the face of which Adele had no response, because Lizette knew how to speak well and raise her voice and bang on the table with her fist, whereas Adele was not a woman of many words, but rather a future chemist of many test tubes.

She wasn't mad at Vita for not being at the discussion about the suitcase, because at that time he was busy paving a road in the Negev: at this rare moment she fought all the powers herself. Luckily he arrived for the vote. Vivienne, Charlie, Rosa, Barbara, Henriette, Bruno, Lizette, Odette, everyone was there, but she lost the suitcase by a single vote, whose she didn't know, of course, since the vote was secret.

This was in 1951. A year and a few months later a "referendum" was held in all the movement's *kibbutzim*, because apparently they hadn't yet invented the Hebrew term. Members were asked if they were for or against the Prague Trials—show trials in the capital of Czechoslovakia, in which most of the accused were Jews. Those charged were accused of a Trotskyist-Titoist-Zionist conspiracy, of serving American Imperialism, and members of the left wing in the *kibbutzim* believed the charges, and were for trials. A part of the members of the Egyptian *garin* were among them: as communists loyal to Stalin the "Sun of the Nations" they were convinced of the Trotskyist-Titoist-Zionist conspiracy serving the Americans, even though two Israelis who had arrived in Prague, one of them from the leadership of the kibbutz movement, were arrested there and also accused of spying against the Soviet Union. Members of the Egyptian *garin* thought that they could vote as they saw fit. They advocated freedom of ideas, or loyalty to Stalin's party, or both things, and didn't know what awaited them.

Only quite soon, after approximately three years as *kubbitznikim*, those who voted in favor of the Prague Trials were forced to leave kibbutz where they had planned to live the rest of their lives. On the bus that transported those exiled to the central bus station in Hadera were twenty-three members of the Egyptian *garin* in support of the Prague Trials, and nearly another sixty of their friends, who joined them in solidarity. Charlie was among neither the former nor the latter, but whoever recalls the dimensions of buses in those years would undoubtedly be amazed and say that they had never before seen such a packed bus. Adele was among the first to get on the bus, and when she turned around saw Tall Lizette get on after her, hair cut short by the hand of an amateur and the suitcase in her hand. Adele approached her, furious.

"Nice change," she said to her.

Lizette chuckled bitterly and said, "I did it myself at night. Joe trimmed it in back. Does it look okay?"

"I would go to a hairdresser so he could go over the spots that are a bit off," Adele said, and added, "but I meant the suitcase."

"Ah, the suitcase," Lizette said. She was around five foot nine. "Everything inside is destroyed. I don't know what they did with it. Apparently they put it in the children's house as a toy closet for their games."

"In the children's house?" Adele was shocked.

They spoke in French.

"They threw us out of the kibbutz, because we violated the collective ideology, and you're still complaining that they put your suitcase in the children's house?" Lizette was angry, "Wake up, Adele. You still haven't woken up?"

Lizette was always a few steps ahead of everyone, and there was no point in trying to argue with her. But how would Adele explain to her mother, who was waiting for her at the central bus station in Tel Aviv, that the suitcase, which was like a wardrobe with drawers, was not in her possession? And if Lizette, with all her height, even just wanders around the central bus station in Tel Aviv and this suitcase is in her hand, it's reasonable to assume that such a special suitcase, being held by such a conspicuous woman, would not escape her mother's attention.

Worried and agitated Adele sat down next to Vita on the bus

to Hadera and related the problem to him in a whisper.

He rose and walked down the aisle and stood next to Lizette and her husband Joe, who were sitting not far from them.

"Where are you traveling to?"

"Tel Aviv," Lizette answer, "Vivienne already managed to find a one-bedroom apartment for us on Shabazi, with a bathroom outside. Where are you going?"

"To my wife's mother's place. In Holon. She lives with a brother of Adele. They just now finished their building. Afterwards we'll see."

"What about work?"

"I'm not worried," Vita answered. He firmly grabbed the leather loop that hung from the rod in the bus's ceiling and leaned to the side, because the bus made a big turn.

Vita was still entirely immersed in the shock of the expulsion. Adele thought how strange this place—the country of Israel—is, where fifty or sixty years came to an end after two or three, but, in truth, she was happy they were done with the kibbutz, even though she knew: her husband was deep in mourning.

"On the way we're stopping at my sister's in Hadera for two or three days," Lizette told him right in the middle of the big turn.

Vita let the bus finish the turn, straightened up, and went back to sit next to Adele with the wonderful news in his mouth: your mother won't see Lizette.

They continued to Tel Aviv on a bus from Hadera. Her mother came to meet her and her Sephardic husband in the central bus station in Tel Aviv. The mother lived with Adele's brother, Freddy, in a new building in a new neighborhood in Holon. Freddy arrived in Israel due to Adele, because he didn't want to leave her alone, but now, when she has Vita, he could travel throughout the world, after finishing flight attendant school. He tried to convince Vita that he and Adele should come live in Holon, but Vita was stubborn. He wanted to live on the edge of the Yarkon because of the bank of the Nile. In Cairo they had a house next to the Nile, on Kasr Al Einey Street, not far from Adele's family's house by Takhrir Square.

Vita wasn't disappointed even when he understood how great the difference is between the Yarkon and the Nile. Around the Yarkon the construction was still sparse and the apartments were cheap, and not long after Vita Kastil succeeded in purchasing a two-bedroom apartment on the third floor on Yehudah Hamaccabi Street at the corner of Matityahu Cohen Gadol, an east-facing apartment that the sun flooded until noon.

After the kisses and the hugs, and at the end of a few obvious questions, the mother fixed her eyes on their pathetic suitcases and asked: "Where's the suitcase?"

Kastil answered her, while his eyes laughed with mischievous kindness:

"It remained at the kibbutz. They wouldn't give it up, despite all their important principles, that's how beautiful it was."

The mother loved her optimistic son-in-law, with the broken expression, and looked at Adele, the daughter who had always been discriminated against unlike her two half-sisters and two brothers, one who was already in Holon, and the older who left for Canada, and out of all of them here she found an extraordinary groom. Bravo, Adele. I don't have to worry about you anymore.

Chapter 3
Vivienne

Vivienne attended the Catholic Immaculate Conception School for girls, Cairo branch. The children of their Armenian neighbors also went there. The school's uniform very much pleased Vivienne. Just by looking at the uniform one saw that this was an excellent school. And they also taught English there, and Vivienne very much liked the English language.

At the school they thought her father was Christian, and he himself, as a Jew and an atheist, didn't care which school his daughter attended. He was an engineer by profession, who always kept a notebook and a pencil in his bag and was interested in bridge construction; some of the bridges he built would be bombed by Israel in time to come. Her mother, who was a pious believer—a thing that led to terrible arguments over religious matters between her and her husband—agreed for her to go to such a Christian school on the condition that she not enter the church there, nor cross herself, and if she had no choice—to cross herself in the wrong direction. Of course Vivienne entered the church, it wasn't possible to avoid that, but she didn't cross herself in any direction.

The uniform was truly beautiful. In the winter a dark blue fleece skirt of good quality, and a shirt of thick fabric in the same color, and embroidered on it in curling English letters: *The Immaculate Conception School*. In the summer they wore a large straw hat with the school's logo, the same skirt, and a cream-colored cotton shirt with a rounded collar.

The teachers were Franciscan nuns, who came on a mission from Ireland. The classes were conducted in English. The nuns also formed a girls' choir that sang in English, and Vivienne was an important participant in it. At one of the rehearsals they praised her in front of the whole choir, telling her she had the voice of a nightingale, and they gave her a soprano solo to sing, in the first row. Later on they gave her many more solo roles, and the nuns treated her like someone who had been given a gift from God.

The nuns' admiration planted enormous pride in her, which was not in keeping with the beatings and belittlement she got from her older brother, as well as some from her mother who was like a shadow walking alongside her first-born son. On the one hand, therefore, the nuns told her she was destined for greatness, and that she would fill concert halls as a singer, and on the other hand, in her home, they told her to sit in silence and not open her mouth, and do what they told her. Perhaps this contradiction, and disappointment at the fact that in the end she didn't fill concert halls but merely bank forms, were the source of the sudden aggressive outburst that characterized her as a grown woman. Inside the cruel melting pot of the state of Israel, as a bank clerk up to her ears in paper, she could go off in a second and start a war with the other clerks, if need be. In her home she conducted a choir of divide and conquer with her daughters.

She went through most years of her life almost without saying *shalom*, not upon entering or upon leaving, because she didn't like to say *shalom* on principle. At home it was obvious that they didn't say *shalom*, but only closed doors, and not always quietly. And at the bank and other places, where she was required to say *shalom*, she forced herself to emit in a silent voice, with utter artificiality, in a language that wasn't her mother tongue anyway: "*shalom* everyone." Afterwards she would sometimes have lengthy arguments over whether or not she did indeed say *shalom*.

To her daughters she didn't just not say *shalom*, rather she started conversations with them using some accompanying term followed by an indirect object, which was in fact the main point from her perspective, that is to say the subject. Sometimes she would begin a sentence with what came after a colon, without mentioning what came before it, as if she expected them to join her stream of consciousness, which after all was the only one in existence. All this made each address of hers to her daughters rather exhausting. Suddenly at times, without any warning, the name of an institution going bankrupt would pop up, or even part of the name of an institution going bankrupt, or the name of a dead person whose clothes were being divided up, or data about the weather in a distant country, or details of shows she saw the night before on television, or the name of an American president who gave a speech—and the rest would be words in a specific sequence out of which it was difficult to construct an event. Vivienne created for them a syntax entirely distinct from the one in which the world was conducted, a kind of singularity sentence with embellishments before reaching the actual subject.

It can't be ruled out that this is the syntax the nuns taught her at school, or that her convoluted manner of expression stemmed from some reshuffling between English syntax, French syntax, and Arabic syntax.

At home the French language ruled, and Arabic and Hebrew went underground. Vivienne taught her daughters recitations in French that she brought from Egypt, such as:

Vive les vacanes,
Point de pénitence,
Les cahiers au feu,
Les livres au milieu.

Charlie and Vivienne lived with the Older Daughter and the Younger Daughter on Nordau Boulevard at the corner of Alexander Yanai, very close to Ibn Gvirol. Vita and Adele lived with the Only Daughter at the beginning of Yehudah Hamaccabi, and they too were very close to Ibn Gvirol, but on its right bank. Both families lived on a fourth, top floor.

In Charlie and Vivienne's apartment the balcony faced west, whereas in Vita's apartment the balcony faced east. Neither of the men could exist without a proper amount of sun. Vita had sun until noon, and Charlie had sun from noon onwards.

The Older Daughter and the Only Daughter were on the round-trip line between the two apartments throughout all the years of their childhood. The Only Daughter very much loved the foods Charlie prepared and came there to fill her lack of sustenance, because at their house there was very strict discipline with regards to what they put in their mouths.

The deaths of the three daughters of Flore Kastil, Charlie's mother, shaped her connection with the son of her old age, who did not get to know his sisters. He would spend entire days with her in the kitchen—so it was until the sorrow subdued her and she was plucked away at the age of fifty. Interesting what remains of her grave in the Jewish cemetery in Cairo.

Flore Kastil taught Charlie how to cook for Shabbat, and how to cook differently for the rest of the week, each day something else. From year to year the spiciness of her foods increased. She taught her son the use of the flame and the importance of cumin and turmeric, but mainly the mighty contribution of black pepper.

Thus the foods that Charlie prepared in Israel were spicy and tasty in a way that could not be replicated. With all his history, he completely took over the craft of cooking in the apartment on Nordau Boulevard. He would stand in the small kitchen with an apron around his waist, and cut and slice and fry and mix, with a severe expression on his face, as if this were an event equivalent to preventing a family catastrophe. Each of his movements toward the drawers, the refrigerator, the flame, were very quick and anxious, and disturbing him was absolutely forbidden.

Sometimes, when he would go out to the balcony while cooking to chain-smoke a few cigarettes, Vivienne would steal into the kitchen and pour part of the sauce into the sink and add water and a bit of sugar, and if Charlie would catch her in the act, he would burst out into terrible screams. Afterwards he would toil for a long time over fixing his dish and would add to it turmeric, mustard, and black pepper.

Charlie and Vivienne's apartment was indeed only a one-bedroom apartment, but it had a giant balcony, wider and taller than that of Vita and Adele. The balcony enjoyed a breeze from the sea, and it was inspiring, because it was on the corner with a commanding view of both the boulevard with its sturdy, flourishing trees, and the smaller street as well, planted with pine trees, where white parasitic mushrooms grew with them symbiotically, at the bottom of their thick trunks. The children would smash them in order to wipe them out, but with no success. They grew back again and again.

The great shortcoming of the apartment on Nordau Boulevard was its lack of a second bedroom, for the parents. They were forced to sleep in the living room, on a bed that opened up out of their domicile sofa. The mattress was too soft and destroyed Charlie's back, and he said, "I have lumbago."

The big western balcony was divided exactly into two, because of a supporting column, and in its corners planters were born, which Charlie nurtured with devotion and rigor. A gardener by the name of Zecharia would come from time to time to prune and fertilize. He was a relative of the singer Shoshana Damari and lived with his mother by the daycare on Amos Street, where the Older Daughter went. His mother was the Queen of Aluminum—she filled their courtyard with aluminum sinks and vessels. Sometimes she would strike them, and the activity at the daycare would fall silent in amazement for some time.

Vivienne and Charlie were of two schools. He was a socialist, and over the years she transformed into an astute trader, who knew how to bargain and wear down her rivals, until they capitulated to her. With her sharp senses she feared the power of capitalism to leave a man lacking everything, and so she saved every penny. The two's greatest fear was going into debt, and since Charlie had a strange urge to buy all sorts of things like shelves, brackets, and Black and Decker power tools, not always necessary, it was decided during late-night conversations that Vivienne would have a monopoly on managing incomes and expenditures, and thus, with the reins in her hands, they would manage to survive and even advance in life, and leave something to their daughters. She for her part gave up on the kitchen almost entirely. The two of them went out with the girls for shopping, except for the purchasing of clothes at cheap outlet stores, which was conducted without Charlie, and sometimes Vivienne bought second-rate clothes, and justly, they were two salaried employees after all—albeit with benefits like vouchers for vacations, and a thirteenth check each year, which they would deposit into a separate savings account.

Their opinions on the fate of the apartment on Nordau Boulevard were as far apart as heaven and earth. Vivienne viewed it as a way station on the path to a two-bedroom apartment with a double bed always open, but Charlie didn't want to leave there for anywhere else.

His life's dream was to receive permission from the municipality to build a room on the roof, and perhaps even to buy a piece of the roof from the neighbors, for another balcony, which he would also fill with planters, and these would get direct sun all hours of the day, in contrast to the planters on the large balcony, which got sun only from noon on. He sat with a sharpened pencil in his hand and sketched out plans for where the spiral staircase of strong wood leading to the room on the roof would be, and how the room would be connected to the open balcony, where it would also be possible to hang laundry that too would get direct sun and dry quickly, without sharing the metal poles for hanging laundry with the neighbors.

And when he got up and began pacing in the living room and counting steps, Vivienne said to him that he had no chance of getting permission from the municipality to build, and that all the neighbors would rise up against him, and they don't need this. He responded to her that it all depended on bribing the right people at the municipality.

In the early seventies he approached, without Vivienne's knowledge, an architect at his work—El Al—who at a major discount prepared for him a serious, professional plan for a room on the roof. The plan, which was sketched out on onionskin, was kept for years in a secretary's drawer, among other folded up onionskins, on which nothing had been sketched, in a special brown folder, kept closed with a black rubber band. In the margins of the sketch, in his beautiful, right-leaning handwriting was written: Nordau.

He tried in vain to appeal to the neighbors' goodwill so they'd agree to let him build on the roof. The neighbors found it difficult to get where the thin, anxious, mustached man was coming from, who returned home at five and on Shabbat hung laundry on the roof and took up all the shared metal poles. He knew well that if he tried to pay off someone at the municipality, that Vivienne would catch him. Therefore he asked his three brothers, who lived in Tiberius, Haifa, and Kiryat Motzkin respectively, to pay off one of the members of the building committee at the municipality instead of him, but the three of them said to him that if his apartment is too small for him, he should move to a bigger apartment.

Real estate prices very much appealed to Vivienne a few months after the Yom Kippur War. In response to Charlie's unwillingness to move from Nordau Boulevard, she bought a two-bedroom apartment in Bat-Yam, approximately two hundred meters from the beach. The apartment was still "on paper"; though they had already starting building it.

She didn't reveal the fact of the purchase to anyone, and on the contract she listed the buyers of the apartment as herself and her two daughters.

Only when the walls of the apartment were already standing strong did she tell Charlie about it, who was speechless with amazement. In her defense she said she assumed that if they had in their possession an existing fact, a large apartment walking distance from the sea in fast-developing Bat-Yam, Charlie and the girls would run to the apartment, because it's new and spacious as well, on the third floor with an elevator.

And so began a new weekly pastime. Every Shabbat Vivienne, Charlie, and the girls would get into the Fiat 600 and go see the progress on the construction in Bat-Yam. Every Shabbat the four would climb up sloping boards in the stairwell still lacking stairs, and go inside the door-less entrance. And then the father and the two girls would receive a detailed explanation from Vivienne: here is your room and this is the parents' room. She prided herself especially on the balcony, which wasn't half the size of the balcony on Nordau Boulevard, but you saw the sea from it. Judging by the wave of construction in the vicinity it was clear that the sea would not remain on this balcony for long.

Charlie told his brother Vita about the apartment in Bat-Yam, and Vita told his wife Adele, who spread the news further—via Bruno, or Lizette, or Henriett—to all members of the *garin*. Vivienne began to be thought of as a real estate shark, and this fact infuriated her, but also flattered her and added some redness to her cheeks.

In front of the members Vivienne denied that she was a "property owner" but Charlie wouldn't help her out of this bind. She said that she bought the apartment for her mother, who asked her for a home in Israel. And indeed, she came from Paris for a while and got too intensely mixed up with the Older Daughter for Vivienne's taste.

The Older Daughter adamantly opposed the move to the apartment in Bat-Yam, and incited the Younger Daughter as well, until the two of them developed a burning hatred toward this apartment.

Over the years the apartment in Bat-Yam became the summer residence for Vivienne's relatives, who would come from France, year after year, for a vacation in Israel.

Before the relatives arrived the whole family would go to

clean and polish the apartment in Bat-Yam, to scrub the floor and shine the stainless steel faucets. They would go up in the elevator with buckets and rags, and spend the Sabbath making the apartment shine. That is to say, the parents—not the girls. They made their way to the nearby beach, which was no longer to be seen from the apartment.

Two or three years after they didn't move to live in Bat-Yam they saw a corner cottage in Ramat Hasharon—a sure candidate for purchase in their eyes, despite the faces the Older Daughter made for them, because the cottage, which had two and half bedrooms, shared one of its walls with the cottage of her Bible teacher, and the Older Daughter refused to see that everything in the world is temporary: today she's her teacher and tomorrow she's her neighbor.

Charlie thought that they found the house of their dreams: ground floor, second floor—and a large garden. No need for flights abroad or for vacations on distant islands. Everything within reach, the garden and the sun. He very much wanted Zacharia the gardener to continue coming to Ramat Hasharon as well. Just to prune and fertilize. The rest of the maintenance he'd do himself. Charlie knew that tranquility would then come to him and he'd be able to stand the difficulties of life and the stress at El Al.

They gave a positive answer to the foreman and returned home to do all the calculations again. But that night there was a significant devaluation of the lira, and inflation consumed the dream.

In the end Vivienne and Charlie purchased a two-bedroom apartment on the third floor in the Bavli neighborhood, and immediately, as is customary, they busted down the wall between the balcony and the living room in order to enlarge the living room, and thus came the end of the era of the balconies. The plants from the balcony on Nordau Boulevard couldn't endure the window boxes in Bavli, even though the sun came from the west there as well. Without the soothing breeze over the heavy summer heat the sun scorched the plants, and only cacti endured there.

Charlie managed to live nine years in the apartment in Bavli. But without the boulevard, without the large trees with the treetops always taking shape, without the wind from the sea, without the small, charming street, without the balcony with its planters, without Zacharia—his life was no longer the same life.

Three giant acacia trees stood in the large lot across from the house and bloomed yellow year-round, and the field beyond the lot would sprout with red poppies, and chrysanthemums and yellow mustard plants. Sometimes sheep would come up to the field from somewhere, and with them a Bedouin.

At the south end of the field was a bus stop for Line 14, which arrived once every half hour and went to the city center. For a few years "missing the 14" would frighten the mother and her daughters, because it meant an annoying walk past the Haifa Road and a tiring wait for Bus 24 or 25, which would arrive from Ramat Aviv packed to the brim.

Today it's clear to Vivienne that the abandoned "Dekel" cinema, from which no one has bothered to remove posters for movies that haven't been shown there for a good many years, will be destroyed one day, and in its place they'll build skyscrapers, a fact that will only increase the price of her apartment, located on the same street in Bavli.

Were she younger she too would hurry to buy an apartment in one of the skyscrapers, in place of her current apartment. All these years she loved the surroundings, and the traffic on Bavli Street, and the respected feeling the housing provided by virtue of being Bavli housing.

The field across the way had already disappeared some time ago, and small buildings had popped up with white mosaic siding in place of sprayed on plaster, but despite the mosaic and the prestige, one could see everything done at the neighbors' across the way. Charlie was no longer among the living when the homes with mosaic filled up the field.

Fifty-two years Vivienne worked at the central branch of the bank, in the city center. She started there as a typist and eventually reached the international division. Even after she retired she continued to work by the hour in the department of credit documentation. But then a new, computerized technological era burst forth, and her joie de vivre, and her jokes, were of no help to her. There was no longer any need for this industrious woman.

Chapter 4
The Grown-Ups

It was an autumn Shabbat at dusk. Most of the leaves on the trees growing along the boulevard had already fallen, and did this over three nights of relentless exfoliation. During the days the street sweepers worked overtime.

From below the members' whistle could be heard, two short ones in a row and one long one—and the entire family came to attention.

Charlie sent the girls to the other room, so they wouldn't roam around their legs, and called Vivienne to come to the kitchen immediately. Both of them put on aprons—he a checkered apron, and she one with a pattern of large flowers.

The whole way climbing up the three flights the members talked loudly amongst themselves. Bruno continued talking even while entering through the open door, which had a fine stainless steel handle, fixed diagonally to a thin metal surface in the shape of a right-angled triangle. Sometimes the door would slam shut and someone would be stuck outside, without the fixed handle able to help him.

There wasn't another man as full of joie de vivre as Bruno Levy. He was the driving force in the group, even though there were among the Egyptian *garin* other driving forces—for instance, Henriette, as well as Odette, Bruno's wife, whose dark hair was short, cut as fashion dictated. Odette was the only one who specialized in the direction of beauty and aesthetics, first she became a hairdresser, and afterwards underwent a course to become a real estate agent, practicing in the Holon area.

More members arrived. All the aluminum folding chairs

were opened, the ones made from interwoven white and faded red plastic wires. The matching table, whose red Formica had faded in the western sun, was opened to its largest. Charlie had already brought a first round of nicely cut hors d'oeuvre from the kitchen, meticulously arranged on the plates.

The members spread out on the balcony, and Charlie opened the asbestos shutters wide, so that the friends could breath the sea breeze and also feel the height.

Vivienne didn't want him to open the shutters, both because of the noise from the boulevard as well as the noise that went out from the balcony—the talking and laughter of the members—which was liable to bother the neighbors. But someone had already said: "What air you have here," and it was clear the shutters would remain open.

The members' children arrived as well, trailing after their parents. Not all of them. But the grown-ups very quickly sent those who did arrive to the other room. There the children were impressed by the new piece of furniture that Vivienne and Charlie had bought for the girls. A library on the top part, and on the bottom part two pullout beds, which when they were folded up inside revealed two writing tables that could be opened if you closed the beds. Two rotating wooden triangles held each table, but always at a slight incline, which didn't let one place a pencil on the table without it rolling and falling off; and books and notepads, if they were wrapped in plastic, would also slide along the Formica surface.

Vita and Adele arrived on foot from Yehudah Hamaccabi Street. Adele again said that it took her seven minutes exactly, and pointed at her expensive watch. At the same time, in the kitchen, Vivienne placed six eggs with extreme care into a pot full of water and lit the middle-sized burner on the white stove with the three flames. Charlie saw that she first filled the pot with water and only afterward placed the eggs in it and admonished her that the order was supposed to be reversed.

"I don't want to see children in the living room, only grown-ups," Bruno called out when someone from amongst the children entered the kitchen while the grown-ups' slogans were flying about.

"We were cosmopolitans," Henriette called out as a continuation of a never-ending argument. "We espoused tolerance, brotherhood, solidarity, and racial equality. Because of this they threw us off the kibbutz."

"Racists," Bruno said, "but along with that they still espouse the idea that all people are equal."

"Only theoretically," Lizette corrected him and chuckled, and most of the members understood as well the hypocrisy she was talking about.

"What do you mean?" asked Odette, who suddenly wanted to work her way into the conversation, but Lizette didn't answer. Ever since she became a teacher of French and English at one of the public schools, she didn't answer everyone, and her opinions also swayed stormily inside herself. In the teachers' lounge she heard entirely different ways of thinking from those of the kibbutz and the Egyptian members, and like all those exiled she developed a complex: don't say a word about the expulsion, except on very rare occasions, and even then only surreptitiously.

The accusation of Anti-Zionism that the kibbutz stuck to them was too great a stain, which could be known about in neither the banks nor the high school teacher's lounge. All told, what happened? thought Lizette, twenty-three members, the Egyptian *garin*'s stubborn core, voted "for" instead of "against," in one of the votes that the national kibbutz movement "recommended" they vote against. How could a vote like this, which was just the expression of an opinion and had no impact on any reality whatsoever, determine fates? Is she the only one who sees the magnitude of the absurdity?

Vita loaded up a second round of hors d'oeuvre on a plate from a set of plates that Vivienne bought on the occasion of a clearance sale at a store near her place of work, the bank's central branch. She actually didn't like the nearby Shalom department store. The items that were in that department store she found for half the price in the nearby streets. When she wandered around from store to store on Herzl Street, Nachalat Benyamin, Grozenberg, Ahad Ha-am, and Lilienblum, she felt joy and always returned home with bags.

The tall and narrow Shalom Tower, for years taller than anything in the city, and the *Davar* newspaper wrote about it being the tallest and most sophisticated office building in the entire Middle East, was built close to the building where she worked, on Achuzat Bayit Street; and when one jumps from its roof there is no going back. Time and again she took the trouble to inform her daughters that someone jumped from the Shalom Tower today, or would respond to the Older Daughter's provocations:

"So, did someone jump from the Shalom department store today?"

"Today no. Yesterday. Thirty-seven years old."

Vita avoided his wife's gaze, because he knew that in her opinion he loaded too much on his plate. Later, at home, he'd pay for this yet, but the taste of the food was wonderful, peppery and spicy like he loved.

He became a big manager at Bank Discount and moved up the ranks, but joy was nowhere near him. They had one daughter, who was a world-class beauty, but at the age of twelve they discovered juvenile diabetes in her, and she became extremely capricious. She would eat what was forbidden, and would perform dangerous experiments on her body.

He sat now next to his good friend Bruno, who worked at Bank Hapoalim. Vita liked Bruno, and over the years, while he himself become more and more silent due to additional disillusionments that life brought on, he saw in Bruno a sort of spokesman. Didyeh started quietly giggling with his wife Nelli. Odette, Bruno's wife, switched hair color every three months, despite the fact that she was already an agent and not a hairdresser, and Vivienne thought she had a screw loose.

Odette tried to ask Charlie how he made one of the delicacies that he and his wife served them, but he ignored her.

Vita chewed hastily in order to manage to taste everything before the big argument waiting for him with his wife began, the argument that might even continue into the night and the following day. There was no way to know. But this was not what would stop him from attacking his mother's tastes inside his brother's foods.

Charlie instructed Vivienne to bring the cut up pickles out to the porch, but got very mad at her for bringing out the tahini before the other pickled foods, which he pickled as his mother had taught him.

In the other room the boredom had already begun to strike the children, and the room looked like Sodom and Gomorrah. All the books and encyclopedias were pulled off the shelves and scattered around the floor and tables, whoever wanted to was immersed in reading, and whoever didn't want to did what he wanted. Even if it was a handstand on the bed with the help of the north wall. The children were thin and happy then.

Bruno's voice overpowered Henritte's, but it was impossible to understand anything. Years earlier, on the kibbutz, the Egyptians were full of enthusiasm and joie de vivre. Now it could be sensed that they strained to sound happy and content. Charlie felt flooded by a deep discomfort. Nothing proceeded like it should. He wasn't pleased by his Sisyphean life: in the morning he runs to work as an accountant at El-Al, and in the evening he returns from work as an accountant for El-Al, and sometimes he remains for additional hours because of problems caused by the company's massive computer, which takes up an entire hall.

On Kibbutz Ein-Shemer, at the start of the fifties, Charlie was half a king. Other than the heavy bundle of keys, with the keys for every shed on the kibbutz, he had access to the stables, and he loved to take out a horse and ride it, but not quickly, and definitely not on asphalt, so the horse wouldn't slip. He avoided grunt work—other than the sheds and the stables, and sometimes the crops, which he loved—and instead cooked piquant meals for the kibbutz, until one day, after the eruption of an altercation between the Egyptians and the old Poles, it was agreed that he'd cook less spicy for the kibbutz, and if the Egyptians wanted, they themselves would add the spices that Charlie bought in Umm al-Fahm to their own portions.

The people of the Egyptian *garin* were known as workhorses on the kibbutz, and worked two shifts, morning and evening. The men worked on D-2, D-4, and D-6 tractors, and both the men and the women stood on their feet for hours and worked in fertilization, harvesting, milking, chicken houses, compost preparation, and there were those who went out from the kibbutz to pave new roads in the new country. Once Bruno got lost on a public works tractor, and even accidentally crossed the border into Egypt, but was immediately located and returned.

Their lives were full of activities. In the evening the people from the Egyptian *garin* would participate in debates with the rest of the kibbutz members, at the end of which were votes. They voted for and against every stupid thing. There was endless shouting and discussion into the night around the question of whether the kibbutz movement was the very heart of the Proletariat—was it the *garin* that would lead the city workers and the industrial workers to a socialist revolution in the Land of Israel, if and when this occurred?

The Egyptians became more and more kibbutzniks, and the more they became kibbutzniks the more they got involved in the idiotic debates that undid Hashomer Hatsair. In their overabundant innocence they took freedom of thought and opinion too seriously, and didn't take into account that it would be inconceivable for a group whose members belong to an identical ethnic group to vote "for" when the kibbutz received instructions from the national movement to vote "against."

After they disobeyed the word of the national kibbutz movement with their vote the rebellious Egyptians were removed from the work schedule. Vita, Bruno, Lizette, and Lazar Guetta assembled at the door of the kibbutz secretary and demanded to know what was the meaning of "this ideological righteousness." Their vote affirmed that they are free and cosmopolitan, and did not at all express that they are disloyal to the kibbutz or the state.

Nothing would help them. The veteran members decided: the Soviet Egyptians sinned by shifting blatantly to the left, toward the "Sun of the Nations"—and therefore they would no longer enter the kibbutz's work schedule, word to the wise.

The Egyptians got the clue and rebelled against the decision. Lazar declared a daylong hunger strike by the entire Egyptian *garin*. Perhaps they thought that they were in Red Square and that the eyes of the world's workers were on them, but in the kibbutz they saw in them a Soviet, Anti-Zionist underground. This is a full-fledged rebellion, they thought there, a rebellion that must be nipped in the bud, without delay.

In short, the veterans were not scared of the Egyptians. They established an expulsion committee, on which two sat—Michkeh the head of gardening, who stood at a height of two meters, and Ignatz the crop man, who was much shorter. Four representatives from among the candidates for expulsion, determined to be strong and to put up a fight, arrived for the committee's deliberations. They still assumed that there was a point in continuing to argue, in the effort to convince the members of the committee that their vote was directed overall against American imperialism, which it's true Zionism is sometimes dragged toward, but they themselves are in no way, shape, or form dangers to the kibbutz or the state. Just the opposite, they constitute an essential workforce, and after all that is why they left Egypt: to contribute to the kibbutz.

But the expulsion committee was not erected in order to not expel. It was satisfied with a practical and purposeful discussion, and arrived at a pragmatic conclusion with regards to the manner of removal from the kibbutz. In a single consultation with Meitek, who was in on the secret, Michkeh and Ignatz decided that each one of the exiled would receive a mattress, bedding, a few objects from the rooms, and one hundred and fifty lira. They left Egypt with more than this, but here the members of the kibbutz still rummaged through their things when they left, in case they took some cup or something else that wasn't given to them.

Yaakov Riftin, born on the kibbutz, was a man of the left who swept the Egyptians behind him, and was himself swept behind Moshe Sneh, who would later have entire streets named after him, without being remembered as a pro-Soviet leader, who would pass sensitive information on to the Soviets. Riftin—in contrast to the Egyptians—wasn't expelled from Ein-Shemer either, but just censured instead.

The expulsion, which Vita defined as a serious mistake, turned the Egyptians into city dwellers with new insights. Many of those who resided in Tel Aviv, or even in Holon, managed to integrate nicely. Others became post-traumatic. The stress of life in the big city and the hard work required in order to make it through the month, caused them bodily tics, mainly in the neck. They would throw their head back, return it forward to its place, cough from the depths of their lungs and spit, while now involuntarily shaking their head no.

No, they are not masters of the land, and it is better for them to shut their mouths and give their opinion to each other only—and not in Hebrew either—on sun-drenched balconies over which darkness slowly descends.

Chapter Five
Tantura

The Only Daughter always said: "My days are numbered, my days are numbered."

She had excruciating pain, and was now freed from it, the Older Daughter thought as she stood before the body. She entered the room in order to get the Only Daughter's large bag and her belongings, and looked at the face of the cousin she admired and saw that she still had a ponytail. She cautiously pulled on the ponytail, and a moment later said to herself, "Damn, she's dead, she doesn't feel a thing," and pulled harder, but cautiously nevertheless. She wandered a bit too much around the body of the Only Daughter, as if she were on Matityahu Cohen Gadol Street in the seventies, and not in Ichilov Hospital in the two thousands. The Only Daughter lay dead. There was nothing more to do.

In the hospital it was customary to leave the corpse in the room for a couple hours, behind a curtain, and afterwards for an orderly to come and take it to the morgue. An hour and a half after the Only Daughter's death her father Vita entered the Department of Internal Medicine with a bouquet of flowers for his daughter. The Older Daughter and Amatsia, the Only Daughter's husband, were waiting for him and hurried over, to prevent him from going to his daughter's room. "A tragedy, a tragedy occurred," they told him together, and he asked, "But what happened?" They were silent and waited for him to understand himself, and when he understood immediately said, "She'll die now," meaning Adele.

But Adele didn't die so quickly. She just went incessantly for medical examinations to find a fatal disease for herself, which would explain to her why she felt the way she felt. There was no medical examination she didn't have, and she was escorted to all of them, in a hired taxi, by her husband Vita, forever loyal to his task. But all the examinations came out okay. She's physically healthy, the doctors said, and gave her more and more pills for depression, but she refused to swallow them, taking only half a Paxil, for anxiety and insomnia.

Once every three weeks, in the late morning hours, Adele and Vita would visit their daughter's grave in Kiryat Shaul. They hired a regular driver, who waited not far from them, in the narrow path that ran between the crowded graves, and left the engine running, because of the air-conditioning. They came to speak with the Only Daughter, but Vita didn't speak, because he knew there was no one to speak with, whereas Adele insisted on talking to her and telling her the news, both the good and the bad, so she'd stay up to date. Vita stood tensed; were she to collapse, he'd call the driver to help him carry her straight to the cab, which would take her straight to the hospital.

He was always the more practical one, compared to his wife and daughter, and when the Only Daughter was still alive and going through a tough time, he would say to her: "Ya'alla, ya'alla, now's Kilimanjaro" or "Ya'alla, ya'alla, now's Everest."

Adele wept leaning on the grave. Vita grumbled and shook his head this way and that. Afterwards he helped his wife clean the grave, during which time he bickered with her about nothing. A tightness pooled in his chest, because he knew what was waiting for him afterwards at home. Crying all day, until he was fed up with his life.

One day, around seven years before her death, this appears to have been in 2000 exactly, the Only Daughter of Vita and Adele asked the Older Daughter of Charlie and Vivienne if she wanted to go with her to Tantura. Vita and Adele were staying in Tantura then with their grandchildren, Levona and Timna, the Only Daughter's two daughters, and the mother wanted to go visit her daughters.

When the Older Daughter was still a girl the Only Daughter would arrange for her to get into the guest houses and convalescent homes where they stayed, because she knew that the Older Daughter didn't have a chance to go to such places. Once, for example, she snuck her into an institution in Ashkelon with a beach nearby, an institution in which people with special diets were hospitalized, and a different friend of the Only Daughter even spent the night there.

One must understand: The Only Daughter was the Older Daughter's pride and joy and a very important artery of hers into life. She learned a ton from her. Like simple information, thanks to the five years separating them, and like that it was possible to escape one's fate, that this possibility existed—provided you're desperate and daring.

On that same day the Older Daughter got really excited, because no one had ever suggested she come to Tantura, and she had never been there.

Interestingly, both of them had natural blond hair with no connection to their parents' hair, probably from the genes of a previous generation, and the blondness very nicely hid their Egyptian origins and bestowed on them a great advantage, even over the Ashkenazi girls in their classes, in elementary school and high school, who had brown hair. During certain stretches they were like sisters. Every Friday, at the home of the Only Daughter's parents and together with her father Vita, they would watch the movie of the week in Arabic on the television's only channel, because over there they were allowed to watch it at regular volume, whereas at the Older Daughter's house they were allowed to watch it only at a very low volume, under Vivienne's supervision.

In the seventies they would go up to the roof of the Only Daughter's house on Yehudah Maccabi to tan, after first bleaching their hair, so that it would be even blonder yet. The Only

Daughter knew what you had to do so that the hair would look natural and was amazing at treating it with the help of hydrogen peroxide and some bluish powder that the owner of the pharmacy recommended to her.

The Older Daughter envied her, because she herself had the look of a skin-and-bones anorexic, whereas the Only Daughter was beautiful, feminine, shapely, smart, amusing, teeming with life, and mischievous. Her juvenile diabetes prevented her from joining the army, but she made up for her lack of patriotism and befriended a few of the new generals who were appointed after the results of the Yom Kippur War. The Older Daughter scowled at this and lost even more weight, but no one paid attention to this other than the IDF, which requested that she add three kilos to herself if she wanted them to agree to induct her.

In order to get to Tantura, the Older Daughter, who was by now already the more vital of the two, had to drive her car. Over the years the Only Daughter grew very ill. Her juvenile diabetes got worse and worse as she left her juvenile years behind. This is apparently the nature of the disease—that it continues after childhood passes, and also prevents the symptoms of childhood to pass: mischievousness, curiosity, adventurousness, and an inexplicable joie de vivre all remain, together with terrible pain in body and soul.

Wherever one placed a finger on her body—she had rheumatic pain. On her legs she had sores that wouldn't close, and her eyes weren't in great shape either, though she could see and read.

She had anorexia during the day and bulimia at night, and all told she was already thin and weak and walked with the help of a cane. She was still beautiful, but her beauty was quite different from that of her youth. Her facial features were sharper, and her brown eyes were deeper set.

The Older Daughter, on the other hand, had gained weight thanks to childbirth, and her condition was better compared to the days when she was a walking skeleton. The sense of humor she once had dwindled, left her like her cousin's calcium. The role reversal between them was quite convenient for her.

She asked the Only Daughter if she was comfortable in the Ford Fiesta, and they were held up some time before the Only Daughter was comfortable. Nadav, the younger son of the Older Daughter, joined the trip as well. He was five years old then.

Throughout the trip on the coastal highway the Older Daughter nevertheless tried to make her cousin from her father's side laugh, but the Only Daughter was sullen. She was in pain and emitted groans, sighs, and complaints. Sometimes the Older Daughter was forced to close off her heart in order to avoid an accident. Her son sat buckled up in the back seat, and she explained to him how her cousin is in pain and suffers badly, but that she'll soon get some medicine and the pain will go away. The boy asked why they have to wait, and the Older Daughter said that the medicine is in Tantura, with her cousin's parents, and so she's doing absolutely everything in order to get there as fast as possible. She talked with him about Levona and Timna, the Only Daughter's daughters and his second cousins, who were waiting for him in Tantura, and how pleasant it will be in the wadi's water, all this while the Only Daughter continued to complain in the background and say, "Oy, God, I can't take it anymore."

In Tantura the Older Daughter found a spot close to the sea and the bungalows and parked the car. She opened the door for her son, who immediately ran to the sea, and then opened the door of the seat beside her, grabbed the Only Daughter's cane, and helped her out of the car.

"Luckily we found a parking spot nearby," the Only Daughter said.

"Luckily," the Older Daughter repeated and held out the cane for her.

The Only Daughter placed her insignificant weight on it and began walking toward her parents—Adele and Vita—who rushed to meet her. A moment after her parents took her, the Older Daughter stood and looked all around. She swallowed up the scene in its entirety and called out with passion and longing:

"Tantura!"

All her life she had heard about this Tantura, which she had never managed to visit. Friends of her parents, who had left Kibbutz Ein-Shemer, would travel to Tantura for the holidays and rent a bungalow by the sea, the way they would vacation in their childhood in Port Said or Lebanon, but Charlie and Vivienne didn't have enough money for Tantura with the three meals included, or perhaps they simply didn't allow it for themselves. By contrast, this time Vita and Adele rented not a bungalow, what they here called an igloo, but rather an actual air-conditioned guest room.

The sand in Tantura was not yellow but white, and there weren't many people on the beach. Nor in the water. The sea looked very clean and deep after only a few steps. There was no breakwater, and therefore there was no pier either. Everyone sat on lounge chairs. Despite the great opportunity for relative happiness—sea, children, sun—a great misery actually nested there. Timna swam in the water and cried nonstop. It was impossible to calm her. Everyone got up in order and tried. Her mother, the Only Daughter, also went into the water up to her knees, even though there was great fear her sores would get infected, and attempted to convince her Younger Daughter to stop crying, or at least get out of the water, so that she herself could then calm her down. But the girl wanted to stay in the water and cry, and this tainted the atmosphere and led to anger toward the girl. Who would have dreamed that precisely then the girl was developing a chronic autoimmune disease of her own, and for this reason was crying in the water?

At noon everyone went into the air-conditioned room and sat down to eat the meal that was brought over from the guesthouse's kitchen. Everyone stuffed themselves except those who had an eating disorder, or had a special diet, such as the Only

Daughter, or had someone who monitored them, like Vita, who could put nothing in his mouth without Adele noticing—in truth the eating of everyone who dined at this meal was disordered, other than the younger son of the Older Daughter, since nothing could disorder his eating.

After the food the Older Daughter left to go sleep, because she was already uneasy from the whole affair. The Only Daughter lay down to sleep as well. Her parents went outside with the children, though not to the sea, but rather to a spot where the children could play and they could talk about the matters of the day with their friends from the Egyptian *garin* who were still alive, and had also come to Tantura.

Immediately after the Older Daughter and the Only Daughter woke up from sleeping the Older Daughter was seized by hysteria and wanted to return right that instant to Tel Aviv. The Only Daughter got annoyed with her, since she possessed the exclusive rights to hysteria in the family, due to her illness, and due to her illustrious past full of hysteria. The Older Daughter rushed the Only Daughter, who told her to relax, but the Older Daughter went out to look for her son who was with the adults from the *garin*. The adults asked what was waiting for her in Tel Aviv that she's hurrying so much, at which point the Older Daughter introduced the decisive point that she knew no one could challenge:

"I don't like to drive in the dark."

Indeed, the point was grasped among the group as *the* legitimate point with a capital "T." Someone even mentioned in French that the father of the Older Daughter, Charlie, may his memory be a blessing, didn't like to drive in the dark either, if her memory doesn't deceive her.

The Older Daughter took the hand of her younger son and returned with him to the room, to check on the condition of the Only Daughter. The Only Daughter told her that she's stressing her out, and that she has more than enough pain and nerves of her own. They talked about five, and now it's only four. There's still a whole hour. But the Older Daughter would not budge: there's liable to be traffic.

The Only Daughter gave the Older Daughter an angry look. She had a very short fuse, only she was already too weak.

Twenty minutes later a small convoy wound its way toward the car. The Older Daughter marched at its head, her son walked behind her, and after him ambled the Only Daughter on her cane.

From afar the Older Daughter already noticed the brilliant reddish, coppery hue of the car's window. Is that the reflection of the sunset? But the sun wasn't about to set, and it was impossible to know what it was causing to happen optics-wise. The sun that was reflected in the car's windshield was reddish-brown, in contrast to the sun in the sky. She looked again at the window and the sun, and wondered as she tried to recall a few laws of physics. The window is transparent, and the sun is still neutral, and so if this is the case how is the reflection crazier than the source? The Older Daughter walked toward her car as if her eyes were glimpsing an ancient wonder. She turned back and said to the Only Daughter: look how beautifully the sun is reflecting on my car's windshield, the windshield's sun is much redder than the actual sun.

And the Only Daughter said: "That's not the sun's reflection. They spray-painted your windows. Didn't you look where you parked?"

Now the Older Daughter saw that they did in fact spray-paint all the car's windows, including the mirrors, in a goldish-brown color, while at the same time making sure not to get any on the body or the plastic enclosing the outside mirrors.

A kibbutz member passed by her and said while walking:

"Go to the convenience store, it's still open, and buy turpentine and a ton of cotton balls. That spot's only for kibbutz members."

"But there's no sign," said the Older Daughter, who was stunned as she examined her vehicle from every angle.

“There’s no sign, because that’s the kibbutz members’ spot. You parked inside the kibbutz.”

“But who would do a thing like this . . .”

“Would you prefer them taking all the air out of your tires? Look, they didn’t touch the body.”

At the store, besides buying turpentine, they told the Older Daughter that she had trespassed on the spot of a jeweler, who’s a captain’s daughter. This captain caught a Nigerian stowaway on his ship and lowered him onto a raft into the middle of the sea.

The store’s turpentine was of no use, and the Only Daughter had already started feeling very bad, but she left her insulin, as usual, in her refrigerator in Ramat Aviv. The Older Daughter ran to call for her uncle Vita, who found an Arab from Fureidis who did the work in fifteen minutes, using water from a kibbutz hose. This too was anathema in the eyes of those kibbutz members who happened to pass by.

Meanwhile the Only Daughter grew weaker and weaker. Her father paid the Arab from the neighboring village, and the Older Daughter and her son and the Only Daughter returned home. This time the Only Daughter still managed to get to her insulin in time, and everything ended peacefully. Afterwards ten more years passed, during which she almost died again and again from excess insulin, or from insufficient insulin. Time after time her husband saved her from certain death, and thus he was called a saint possessing supernatural powers, because sometimes he came home at an unusual time, not knowing what was pushing him to return, and thanks to this she survived.

One night, almost at the end of the ten years, she sat alone in the kitchen and ate brownies nonstop. When she left the kitchen full of satisfaction she made a mistake in her calculations and injected herself with too much insulin. Early in the morning her husband heard her breathing heavily and saw that she was unconscious. He called for an ambulance, and again paramedics filled the beautiful house in Ramat Aviv, and the two daughters woke from their sleep in a panic. They took her to the emergency room, and there she spent three weeks on a respirator. Everyone thought she was done for, but then she woke up and immediately wrote on a piece of paper: "Jeu de Paume," the name of the museum in Paris that she thought still exhibits Impressionist works. For a few more days she continued only writing, until very slowly the ability to use her voice returned to her—but the voice that came out of her wasn't her voice, but instead a very hoarse voice, because of all the tubes that had been inserted down her throat while she was on the respirator.

The last time she was hospitalized—from which she didn't return—there was no call to an ambulance involved. The Only Daughter called the Older Daughter and told her than they were heading to the hospital because she was having rheumatic pains in her leg, and since the Older Daughter wanted to know first, here she's letting her know. She was still very hoarse, and her voice was heartrending.

The Only Daughter was a kindhearted woman. Since the Older Daughter was competitive in terms of her position in the family, which always seemed fragile to her, the Only Daughter informed her that she was headed to the hospital before informing the others. They would meet up *there*.

They admitted her into the Department of Internal Medicine, gave her shots for the pain, and performed inhalations on her. The Older Daughter—who we'll continue to call this since despite her more than fifty years she still hadn't built for herself a complete identity beyond her family and saw herself mainly through the eyes of her mother Vivienne, and still hoped to win full recognition from her—and so, this same dependent soul, the Older Daughter, would come to the Only Daughter in the morning, and would bring her a cappuccino from the café downstairs, and saw her dying, and in her heart said—let her die, take her already, she's suffering so much, do her a favor and take her. She suffered from excruciating pain, the Older Daughter wanted to inject her with morphine herself, and afterwards a nurse could come and finish the job. The Only Daughter was still hoarse, and called the Older Daughter "Dear," something she had never done: it was clear as day that the end was near.

On Thursday her sugar was high, but the nurses said that they know, yes, they know, and didn't give her insulin. Why not give insulin to someone whose sugar is six hundred? Unclear. Her husband wanted to inject her himself from their personal insulin, but when he did this the week before the nurses screamed at him that he was liable to kill her. He's not a doctor, don't dare touch her. The Older Daughter went back and forth to the nurses and the doctor, and again and again said her sugar is dangerously high today, and that there could be irreversible consequences if they didn't inject the patient with insulin—but she knew that it was best not to fight for the life of the Only Daughter, one must instead take advantage of the system's powerlessness. And so, the next day, on Friday at noon, the phone rang in the house of the Older Daughter, and the husband of the Only Daughter said to the Older Daughter: "It's over." The Older Daughter burst out screaming, and frightened neighbors knocked on the door to ask what had happened.

Chapter 6
Elementary School

Charlie and Vivienne sent the two girls to the A.D. Gordon School, named for the great Labor Zionist leader. This was a school for workers' children, who learned there until five to one, ate lunch until one-thirty, and then did homework until four. In short, the children were stored within its confines for the maximum time.

A neighborhood school on Lassalle Street, between Ben Yehudah Street and Yarkon Street, very near the waterfront. On Ben-Yehudah, next to an expensive carpet shop, one could buy round, blue-colored gum from a woman of Persian extraction, like the rugs.

Lunch at the school was reasonable and poor. The socialist-Zionist ideology was the school's guiding principle, but a Jewish touch was also maintained there through different sorts of prayers, whose addressees were never clear. Were it not for the Judeo-Christian background she received at home, the Older Daughter would have been liable to think that she was an idol worshipper.

In those days, the days of the Cold War, there were those in Israel who moved more to the left than the left, and the children of parents who already in those days thought the two states for two peoples was an inevitability studied at the school. In fact, this was almost the school's fashion, but this doctrine was balanced out by means of a flood of Land of Israel songs at every available hour of the day under the instruction of the music teacher Meir Mor, who played the accordion and rained terror down on all the students and it appears on himself as well. No wonder: throughout the entire Second World War he hid in a hole.

No boy or girl dared to stand up to Meir Mor, because of what he went through, and every time he hung the accordion on his chest, about two hundred upper-level students at the school (those between fourth and eighth grade), were forced to burst out in song, those who wanted to and those who did not. For instance, every day in the cafeteria, before lunch; and a full hour every Sunday morning, to start the week off on the right foot.

For Vivienne, as a working mother, the whole arrangement of until-four-in-the-afternoon was very convenient. Charlie ate lunch at the airline's kiosk, the girls ate lunch at school, and she herself was satisfied with a sandwich she got from the woman who brought around tea. Thus there was no need to set a table at home even once a day, because dinner could be light and in front of the television. If there was one thing Vivienne hated in our world, other than a few other things, why it was setting a table—because of the cleaning one needed to do afterward, she explained.

Vivienne would return exhausted at three-thirty from work at the bank downtown, with a headache that expressed itself with distress in body and soul, and she would immediately take a pill. Charlie—who in his heart was a peasant, or shepherd, who needed only a flute and book in hand—would be transported home by El-Al at exactly a quarter to five. In the three-quarters of an hour Vivienne was left with between the moment the effect of the pill was felt and Charlie's arrival, she had to straighten up and clean the house. Woe is her if she wouldn't manage. The man doesn't understand that she worked all day at the bank and didn't sit with legs crossed at home. But she polishes only what is possible.

Until fifth grade the Older Daughter was responsible for the Younger Daughter returning home safely. And in sixth grade, right when she was freed from this task, a new girl arrived in her class, with very long loose hair, and the Older Daughter became her close friend. The new girl was lively and vivacious, and from time to time would break something, once an arm and once a leg, and then they would call for her mother, and her mother also had long loose hair. The girl always refused to put her hair up, even in gym class, and she had steady bitter arguments about this with the gym teacher, but the main issue was the breaking of arms and legs. Then the new girl would remain at home long weeks, spending the days in bed and missing out on classes, and the Older Daughter would bring her assignments home and keep her up to date, and as such the family of the long-haired girl considered her a wonderful, loyal friend, a real angel on earth—something that would forever please the Older Daughter and provide her relief from her doubts over her right to exist. For the sake of the truth, the Older Daughter was born after the death of the ***true*** Older Daughter, who died a few hours after birth—so Vivienne said—because she was too small. In her childhood the Older Daughter heard about the other Older Daughter and concluded from this that there exists something problematic surrounding her very right to exist. Over the years the Older Daughter who died transformed into "the first Older Daughter," whereas the second Older Daughter became just "the Older Daughter," and the Younger Daughter was always and ever "the Younger Daughter."

The long-haired girl was the Younger Daughter in her family. Her and her mother's long hair was brown. Her middle sister had regular length brown hair, and her older sister had short brown hair. All the sisters as well as the mother used the popular conditioner Kroiter. Its scent followed after them, and the large green bottle stood out in each one of their apartment's three bathrooms.

The three sisters were crazy about the Older Daughter's first name because of its simplicity. They had the rarest of Canaanite names, which barely appeared even once in the Bible. And even though these names were intended to accentuate the difference between them and the uniqueness of each one, the rareness of their names actually made them resemble each other. It was clear that their parents investigated the Concordance for the Bible at length before choosing the name for each and every one of them.

Until then the Older Daughter didn't think it was possible to devote so much effort to something as insignificant as the giving of a name to a child, and in addition to this, they called her by such a beautiful name. She really wasn't used to such individual address, because she always saw herself as a piece of the family—a piece that in general was not easy to separate from the whole. But here, personal attention was possible even in our world, and only a few streets from her home, among the family members of the girl with the long hair, those users of Kroiter from the tall green bottle. Despite their voting for the right and for Greater Israel candidates, they treated the Older Daughter like a person unto herself, and not like a walking broom, as she was called more than once, and this was an entirely new and confusing development.

At their place she was also asked for the first time in her life if she was a relative of the painter Kastil, because they had a painting of his in the living room. The Older Daughter felt nothing for the painter or for the painting—despite her efforts. At her house, at the end of Nordau, her father divulged from behind his mustache, while cutting onions, that the painter is a distant cousin, and at one of the opportunities she mumbled something to the family of the long-haired girl about her family history and noticed the strong impression her words made on the father of this family—Yehoshua, a tall, thin man, who loved to talk about his studies at Oxford, and it was never possible to know who was truly listening to him and who was just being quiet.

The Older Daughter deeply loved the family of the three sisters with the rare biblical names. She loved the mother too, who easily got angry because of rising and falling sugar, but was extremely kind, and the father too, who welcomed her into the family's lap as if it went without saying. She loved to stay at the house on Yarkon Street, a house that was a step up in her eyes.

There was a closet that was used as a partition between the living room and the kitchen and that opened on both sides: on one side was silverware for guests, and on the other side was a hiding place for chocolates and nuts of all sorts. And everywhere the opposite of suffocation—they would knock on the door before entering a room there.

Due to the very fact of staying there she was exempt for all the days of her life from the need to climb the social ladder. They were people of the "Freedom" party and voted for Begin, and the Older Daughter did indeed feel freedom in their house, felt it and how. First, what space! They had a giant apartment that was created out of two apartments that had been connected together. The Older Daughter had never before seen anything like it. The oldest daughter had a purple room, and for this purpose they brought in a special designer. How much she learned from them. Entire meals without bread. A cloth napkin for each meal, folded into a beautiful shape under its cutlery, and sometimes the cutlery was silver, an inheritance from the grandparents, but the festive silverware was in her eyes actually less beautiful that the daily, which sparkled because they cleaned it in a dishwasher that ran on electricity with powder from Switzerland.

And what an embarrassing thing she did once! The mother, who was good-hearted but mentally damaged, and did everything in her ability to ingratiate herself with everyone, put out her hand to her so that she'd pass her plate to her, but the Older Daughter thought that she wanted to "slip her some skin"—in the language of the time—or to "give her five"—in contemporary language—and she gave her five back.

She was thirteen years old then.

Between the first and second course the mother would light a cigarette, and around the table they'd talk about Kafka, and everyone participated in the conversation. And it also turned out one could order a home pedicure. No need going to the School for Cosmetics in Holon.

The Hebrew they spoke there was different, different from

that taught at school as well, and in general, something else there stirred under the surface. The house was full of books, but books in Hebrew, and some of them were new; for example, *The Flea Circus*, and other titles she hadn't heard of. Woe unto her if she were to say "Stalin" in this house, but on the other hand, they sent the long-haired to a school where there were teachers who would sometimes switch the statue of A.D. Gordon in the dining hall with a statue of Stalin, even after his horrors were discovered; the "Freedom" people sent their girl who was used to eating gourmet to a school with a workers lunch. The girl didn't get along in the previous school, and so they moved her to A.D. Gordon, known for its openness to all kinds of children, and the girl got revenge and broke limbs.

The large apartment was managed by a worker named Rami. A tall man, who got into debt, and had now learned his lesson and paid them back. The Older Daughter and her friend also saw him sweeping the city streets, and then they would ignore him, but at her friend's house they used to talk with him about this and that. The Older Daughter also ignored him when she met him in the street alone, because she understood that this was customary. One time, on Dizengoff Street, she nonetheless said hello to him, but he didn't answer.

The Older Daughter saw in the members of this family people who knew how to live right. They moved from "Freedom" to "Liberals," and their freedom grew further in the eyes of the Older Daughter, because it had now become universal. At meals they would laugh from what one said to the other and not at what one said to the other, that is someone would say something and the other would laugh as if the first told a joke. And sometimes a joke would be told—someone would say: "Listen to this joke . . ." and then would speak for many minutes, and everyone would listen without interrupting.

They owned a chocolate factory, which would provide chocolate spread of one quality to the IDF, and of a different quality to the most select bakeries across the city. In their large Westinghouse refrigerator there was always a large cake with frosting, which one of the bakeries would send to them. Sometimes there were two different cakes, and sometimes even a third, and they were sliced in advance. The Older Daughter would then receive three slices, a slice from each cake, exactly like her friend with the long hair. During the periods when the friend had a broken arm or leg, and she couldn't run outside and go wild with all the energy she had, she would be very aggravated, and the members of her family praised the patience of the Older Daughter, who would spend hours in their home day after day, the main thing being not to go back to her own house. The Older Daughter didn't know it was possible to praise someone like that, and even more so herself. And all this was very convenient, because the person with the long hair lived on Hayarkon Street almost at the corner of Nordau Boulevard, across from Independence Park that was behind the Mediterranean Sea. All that separated them was the beautiful boulevard. And the Older Daughter was slim, skinnier than Twiggy, and her legs were long and thin, and her steps were long. The distance was also so short, and the trees so lofty and so exquisite, and raised her spirits, such that neither boredom nor emptiness descended upon her suddenly. The Older Daughter logged a lot of kilometers round-trip along the beautiful boulevard.

The dining hall at school was a large rectangle, at whose end a bust of A.D. Gordon's head, neck, and shoulders stood on a pedestal. The long and narrow tables were arranged in two lines, and there were no chairs, but rather only spartan benches. In the center of the table stood a bowl into which the children emptied the food they were sick of, before moving on to the next course on the same plate. The idea for this bowl, which was called a "kolboinik," the school drew from kibbutz dining culture. These days those "kolboiniks" have already disappeared, and "kolboinik" turned into a nickname for a jack-of-all-trades, or for someone who fills various positions and moves from one to another based on the need.

There was order in the school. Before they gathered in the dining hall Tzvi the principal hit a gong three times, to announce that the time was five to one. Where did this gong come from? Was it really an ancient gong from China? No one asked and no one knew. Following the sounds of the gong the children entered the dining hall, and after sitting down on the benches along both sides of the long tables, they first, of course, broke out in song to the sounds of the music teacher's accordion, and after singing the principal would read aloud the school's newspaper, which was called "Everyday Tales," in his voice scorched from cigarettes.

A hush would fall over the dining hall during these minutes. The children were obedient, and Tzvi read without coughing or clearing his throat.

One day during the week would be dedicated to manual labor, because Gordon's doctrine apparently was the school's top priority: work and learn. But in practice all sorts of different and strange ideologies swarmed around there, and it was hard to fathom the teachers' innuendos.

On workdays the class would be split up. A third of the students would learn carpentry or sewing, with no distinction based on gender; a third would go to a farm to work in agriculture; and a third would learn home economics, that is the main food groups and their importance, as well as cooking. This day of the week was known as a day off, since there was no need to do homework before it, other than home economics, where there was usually an easy question to answer in writing such as, what are proteins. But most of the students didn't answer, because they would be swept away in the rest of the class's current of inactivity.

The rumor was that the home economics teacher too was in the Holocaust, and the children were very scared of her. It was already customary at that time to fear those who were in the Holocaust, because there was no knowing what to expect from them. The teacher was very tough, but she wasn't a bad person. One could know this according to her punishments. Parents slapped their children if they said at home that this teacher learned from the Gestapo. There were homes where it was forbidden to say the word Gestapo at all. Everyone respected the home economics teacher and there was no chance to complain about her. Even the homeroom teacher would close her eyes if they came to complain to her about the home economics teacher, as if there was nothing to be done—one had to absorb her abuse after the abuse they gave her.

Thirty-five years later the long-haired girl—who all these years later still had the same hairdo, and only trimmed the ends from time to time, and other than a few gray hairs still had dark, thick, brown hair—decided to banish the Older Daughter from her circle of acquaintances.

She didn't arrive at this decision all at once. It was clear that the final incident, on the heels of which she announced her decision, was merely the straw that broke the camel's back.

For twenty-some years the relations between the two faltered, but they dragged it behind them in remembrance of the good times. And here the long-haired invited her to lunch one Shabbat, and the meal was attended by important Israeli personages and a few other celebrities, among them balding people with ponytails made from what was left, people with buzz cuts according to the fashion of their children, even though their hair was thin and silvery.

Never before had the long-haired made a social gesture like this and brought the Older Daughter into contact with her people. The two always met tete-a-tete, and the conversation between them was conducted out of mutual respect for tradition and with the expectation that some miracle would perhaps occur.

At that pioneering Shabbat lunch the Older Daughter did not flow with the conversation, and the things that she divulged on that occasion were not connected to what was being talked about in the conversation, and thus she demonstrated social irresponsibility and a disproportionate otherness. Following that meal the long-haired decided to banish her, and so she did.

But only after the fact, during a phone call a few months later, did she announce this to her ex-friend, and elaborate that it was all because the Older Daughter was unable to integrate fluidly into the conversation that was conducted at lunch on that lovely Shabbat, nor could she take pleasure like all the guests in the lamb from Chinawi the butcher, or in the long-haired's husband's story, how he obtained it at a lower price than normal, nor did she enjoy his story of how he obtained some fruit, or perhaps chestnuts, from an Arab in the third alley over from the flea market in Yaffo at a ridiculous price. While her husband was telling about the Yaffo adventures the Older Daughter rose from her seat and bent over the built-in bookshelves, and removed a book by Oscar Wilde, and didn't even read it, just flipped through it, and upon noticing that the act annoyed everyone she immediately closed the book and came back to listen to the husband, but it was already too late.

During one of the home economics classes the Older Daughter and her long-haired friend sat next to each other like best friends. There was nothing broken in the friend that day, all her limbs were fine. The home economics teacher paced back and forth in the classroom and looked for someone to descend upon, and yes, she located the Older Daughter, bent forward over her notebook and flipped through it to see if this one had answered the question "What is a carbohydrate?"—no. She hadn't answered. Under the question that she had written in the previous class and marked with a red line was a blank page. The home economics teacher bent forward more, her glasses fell down a bit to the bump on her nose, and the tip of her nose nearly touched the Older Daughter's notebook, and then, from this height (the two of them, the standing and the sitting, were now at the same height), the teacher turned her face to her and asked, while she stood straight up:

"How much homeworrrrk did you have for today?"

The question was rhetorical, and her "R" rolled like always, because of her country of origin. And like always the home economic teacher was not satisfied with one time, but rather paced toward the board and on the way asked another student, "How much homeworrrrk did you have for today?" and then turned around, made another pass, and asked the entire class, "How much homeworrrrk did you have for today?" A giggle passed through the class, and the long-haired friend shook her head, and the home economics teacher continued walking while checking the zipper of her dress, and then a sharp shriek sliced through the air and froze the home economics teacher on the spot.

The hair of the long-haired friend was caught in the teacher's zipper. This was a thick, stubborn zipper, one of those that they would sew on at home, and today are no longer in use. Even the sewing and embroidery teacher who was summoned was unable to separate it from the hair of the long-haired friend. It is impossible to describe the girl's cries and her protests against everyone's efforts to calm her. There was nothing left to do except call the principal so he could phone the owner of the hair's mother.

The mother who arrived insisted that they cut a slice of the zipper, or even the dress, and she would go with her daughter to an expert, who would gently remove the hair, but the home economics teacher said angrily that nothing would happen if they cut a lock of this spoiled girl's hair, It'll grow! It'll grow back! Is this not a country of Jews! At the sound of these things the girl went back to shrieking horribly, and her mother said to her: "Don't worry, don't worry," and promised the teacher ten dresses in place of the current dress, but the teacher too was more than a little stubborn.

"I told her to cut it short," the mother said. "To wear it long in high school. In high school they wear it long. I wore it long in high school. In primary school you don't wear it long. Here, look," the mother pointed at the Older Daughter, whose hair was curly blond, and not especially short, "her parents know. They are native Egyptians, but at home they speak French. The Egyptian are something different from the rest of the Orientals."

The friendship between them lasted many more years, yet without the presence of her parents in the vicinity it faded more and more, until it came to an end during that Shabbat lunch. It's clear that the long-haired invited the Older Daughter because she wanted her to talk about this and that with the same freedom with which she would speak in her childhood home, but the Older Daughter was speechless. She just couldn't. The conversation was worthless and dealt with various boasts. Someone from among the guests confessed that he takes Viagra even though he doesn't really need to, and in spite of this his sex life has improved and as a result his quality of life in general. Someone else pointed out that he too takes Viagra for the exact same reason. The women laughed and volunteered information from the bedroom. The men were pleased by their wives' open manner of speaking. The long-haired directed a sharp, angry stare at the Older Daughter. Her control of the event as a guest slackened. It wasn't pleasant for her that her teenage daughters were also sitting at the table and listening to the conversation. Her old friend scowled when she revealed that people who buy meat at Chinawi also have a steady sex life, and the long-haired looked at her as if they were already strangers.

The sewing and embroidery teacher eventually succeeded in separating the zipper from the long-haired's hair and only a few lost hairs remained poking out from the zipper.

Everyone sighed in relief, other than the Older Daughter, who actually wanted something to get cut today: the dress or the hair. When the class went back to the home economics lesson (only the owner of the long hair was taken home), and the teacher continued teaching about carbohydrates, the Older Daughter fell into a depression the beginning of which was a disappointment over the fact that the routine again prevailed. The teacher wrote the homework on the board: answer the question what are fats, and said that in another two weeks there would be a test on all the food groups.

Chapter Seven
Revolution

ONE COULD FEEL in the air that a revolution was approaching. The white gold—cotton—workers held major strikes, and the other Egyptian workers were fed up too. Demonstrations broke out, which were crushed with a very strong hand, and the leaders of the strikes and demonstration were thrown into prison and tortured.

Only the peasants, who lived in clay huts, always said, "*Maktub, maktub*," it's written since it didn't occur to them that there existed on the surface of the earth a different way of life, less arduous and less determined in advance. They continued drinking water from the canals that transported the Nile's water, despite the schistosomiasis; their children had trachoma, and the adults were stricken with kidney diseases and died young.

The visits by the young members of *Hashomer Hatsair* from Cairo among the peasants along the Nile were meant to prepare the youth for kibbutz life. They encountered there, for the first time in their lives, plowing, fertilizing, sowing, and the growing of vegetables. The emissaries from Israel did tell them that on kibbutz everything is different, but nevertheless the heads of the movement also wanted the Egyptian youth to bring "something of their own" with them from Egypt.

These visits threw Vita Kastil for a loop and gave rise in him to different insights, not necessarily agricultural. He couldn't believe that the peasants lived this way. Without bathrooms, without electricity, without running water. On these visits Vita was burdened with great suffering.

Now he sensed deeply the meaning of the gap between the

poor and the rich, and what corruption, injustice, and discrimination were, and what the class war that Karl Marx spoke about was. As an Egyptian he started to take part in the tough demonstrations against Farouk's monarchical regime, and as a Zionist he smuggled Jews out of Egypt. Both things he did at risk to his life.

Most young members of *Hashomer Hatsair* in Egypt did not go to these protests against King Farouk. Mainly Vita went, and sometimes dragged his brother Charlie and his good friend Bruno with him. But above all Vita was responsible to responsibility, and thus would send his younger brother home before it got too dangerous, or he would intentionally lose Bruno and continue on with the river of people toward Ismailia Square (today—Tahrir), where the battles with the police and the army mainly occurred.

One day a particularly large demonstration took place, which set out from Cairo University and transformed into a surge of people moving toward Ismailia Square. Vita had pockets filled with marbles of all sizes, and when he fled from the police, he dropped them behind him. The cops stumbled on them, but mainly it was the cavalry horses that slid all over them.

He fled via the Abbas Bridge—a bridge over the Nile whose two sections would rise straight up in order to allow ships to pass. When he was on the bridge, with hundreds of other protesters, the police began to raise it. Protesters rolled down the inclines of both sections and fell into the hands of the police and the army, who waited for them below and beat them furiously with batons. Others hung from the two raised sections, and the army shot at and sometimes hit them, and they dropped into the water. Hundred fell or jumped there, and most of them drowned. There were protesters who swam from the banks to the heart of the river in order to save those who were drowning.

Vita grabbed the rusty iron of the raised bridge's railing and remained hanging in the air. The palms of his hands that held on grew whiter and whiter and lost their strength. He had no choice left but to jump. He estimated that he was looking at a jump of about sixty feet. The bridge was already almost perpendicular to the Nile. He saw that other people, above him and below, were jumping into the water. There were those who made fun of the whole thing and dove head first, as if they were in the Olympics, and not candidates for slaughter.

He assumed that jumping to the water from such a height was equivalent to jumping onto a concrete surface. Below he saw boats collecting the people who had jumped.

"Maktub," he said and freed himself from the bridge.

The fall was brief but intense and unforgettable. His head wanted to fly backwards, to disconnect from the rest of his body, but he tried to protect the nape of his neck with his hands and pull it and his shoulders forward, only instead his whole body then began flying uncontrollably in every direction. He tried to maintain some center of gravity, but from nature's perspective this was a fall like any other: whether you were talking about a person or a stone, it was all the same.

In the water his awareness began operating again, and he paddled upward with eyes wide open, though he saw nothing beyond murkiness and bubbles. Some seaweed stuck to him, and he struggled not to swallow water. When he reached the surface of the water and his breathing returned to him, he noticed one of the protesters swimming toward him. This young Egyptian man instructed him to swim toward a small boat. A bullet that missed him danced along the water's surface. Vita wasn't much of a swimmer, but at this moment he forgot that fact and swam with all his might at the young man's command. He looked back, to Vita beating and paddling in the Nile's thick water, and called to him: "Ya'alla, ya'alla, Kilimanjaro!"

Only after the two were lifted up into the boat, and waited for a few additional youths who swam toward it, did Vita notice the bodies floating all around. Despair seized him. The fact that he remained alive after jumping no longer made him happy. But the young man, who sensed him weakening, called out to him again, "Ya'alla, ya'alla, Kilimanjaro!"

This call became his personal motto, and he even built on it with what he remembered from geography class. At the Katawi Pasha Elementary School Vita was a student thirsting for knowledge, who especially loved history and geography. Afterwards, at the commercial high school, the history teacher, Monsieur Habib, gave him free access to the library and recommended books to him. He would sit for hours in the library, and would take books home, and once Misyeh Habib even loaned the globe out to him for a few days, and Vita studied it thoroughly.

And thus he had his provisions: To his right stood Kilimanjaro, Everest, Mont Blanc, Ojos del Salado, and Aconcagua, and to his left—"Maktub."

At the end of his life, in Ward C, they asked him his name, and he answered suddenly: David, even though that was his father's name. He was entirely lucid, and said again, "Write David. My name is David Kastil."

On his identity card the name "Emil" too was written, because that was what he was called in the forged documents with the help of which he left Egypt. But he didn't like this name, even though at Bank Discount, where he wound up in the end, they actually loved the aroma of the name "Emil," and they used it even after his death, in the condolence notice published by the bank's management. But in the family's announcement he was called Victor—Vita's full name according to his wife Adele.

The eulogy for her uncle read by the Older Daughter in the eulogy plaza in Kiryat Shaul was printed on orange paper. Later her sister, the Younger Daughter, said wonderful things about his gray forelock, and his mustache, and his kindhearted smile, and about the confidence he always inspired in those around him.

And then Tzvi Tirosh, Vita's good friend and confidant, one of the people who was the nucleus of the Egyptian *garin*, went up to the dais and addressed the young generation and spoke about Vita's resourcefulness, as a fighter for Egyptian justice, as an activist in *Hashomer Hatsair*, who risked his life and smuggled Jews out of Egypt with forged passports. This was after the establishment of the State, only he didn't necessarily smuggle them to Israel, but rather to other countries, such as France, Canada, and Argentina, because he didn't like classifying the candidates for *aliyah*, a task which *Hashomer Hatsair* imposed on Doctor Marzuk, the same Marzuk who Nasser executed in 1955, without taking into consideration the fact that his mother was his, Nasser's, wet nurse in his infancy. The doctor arranged thorough testing for all the candidates, and only the healthy ones capable of performing hard work were selected for smuggling into Israel; the others were left for the time being in Egypt.

Tzvi Tirosh's address to the young generation was moving, especially in light of the fact that there were between three and five people who could be called "the young generation." He asked them not to forget Vita's work and courage, who on the one hand participated in the protests against Egypt's worthless regime, and on the other hand arranged immigration for tens of thousands of Jews to every end of the earth under the auspices of *Hashomer Hatsair*, and was thus the most daring of the group. And he also worked on the ground. He would go and knock on doors in *Haret Al-Yahud* and convince the parents to place their children in his hands, because he managed in one way or another to obtain forged passports for them. He escorted them all the way to the ships, before the eyes of the Egyptian police!

Tirosh next mentioned Vita's great spiritual strength, a strength that was severely damaged by the death of his Only Daughter four years before his own death. He told the young generation that for the last twenty-five years of her life the Only Daughter was in and out of hospitals, and during the trying, painful, horrible examinations, and in the face of all sorts of obstacles she had to overcome, Vita would say to her: "Ya'alla, ya'alla, Kilimanjaro! Ya'alla, ya'alla, Everest!" And thus extended her life by at least ten years. He would prod himself too as long as she was alive: "Ya'alla, ya'alla, Mont Blanc! Ya'alla, ya'alla, Ojos del Salado! Ya'alla, ya'alla, Aconcagua!" And right when he ran out of tall, important mountains, he would start the list all over again.

Tirosh forgot to mention that in between the tall mountains Vita would also repeat to himself and his daughter: "*paciencia*." Every time in his life that he encountered some absurdity, some intimidating difficulty, he would say *paciencia*, and sometimes laugh as well, due to the difficulty's intimidation.

After his daughter passed away he stopped with Kilimanjaro, but to Adele, his broken wife, he said a few times: "Maktub." Yet Adele refused to be convinced and continued to speak to the Only Daughter as if she were alive. This matter was very hard for Vita, because he didn't believe in communing with ghosts. He said *paciencia* to himself often during those four years between her death and his.

He was buried not far from her, the last of the five brothers.

Chapter Eight
Year of the Pig

ALL OF US have heard and learned about the Spanish Expulsion. In the year 1492 the Spanish crown decided to separate once and for all the Jews and the Conversos (surely they were Marranos, whom they would deal with afterward). And thus the Spanish crown also separated the Muslims and their Marranos, the Moriscos.

In many books writers went out of their way to narrate the great tragedy of the Jews in the fifteenth century—the Spanish Expulsion and the consequent expulsion from Portugal. Hundreds of pages were written about the Marranos, who hid their Jewishness and were allowed to remain in their countries, but were not spared from the Inquisition's persecution. And on the other side, detailed descriptions of the exiles' tribulations and hardships, their loss and heroism, were written. The route of their wandering and their successful or unsuccessful efforts to settle in other places were typically detailed there.

Yet it is hard to believe that one unique perspective of the period, that of Jonathan Tzadik from the University of California, Berkeley, has occurred to anyone other than him.

In an article that Tzadik disseminated through the Internet in the first decade of the third millennium, he explained and proved that the year 1492 was the year of the ***pig*** in Spain. He did not detail when the year of the pig was in other kingdoms besides Spain, nor when in Spain, or in all the other countries that existed in the world then, was the year of the fox, the year of the raccoon, or the year of the owl. His conclusion was valid only for the pig, and only in regards to the Spain of that year.

In the decade that began in 1492—wrote Tzadik of Berkeley—Spain vomited up from its innards the two great enemies of the pig who lived in it, the Jews and the Muslims.

And thus, Tzadik saw things accurately, but what a twisted mind he has.

We must remember that when Spain was Muslim, the hairy, dark-brown Iberian pig was anathema. One was forbidden to raise it, and it was raised and eaten only in isolated monasteries, in godforsaken places.

The scholar from North America offers an additional piece of data: in the year when the Jews were exiled from Spain Columbus also set out on the journey in which he reached America. And what did he take with him? He took eight Iberian pigs with him, which he left on the new continent. In the end these pigs multiplied throughout America, and together with the discovery of the spicy red pepper brought about chorizo as well, which enabled the nutritious, inexpensive meat of the pig to reach even the lower classes.

The following incident took place as well that year, or a year later, two years at most. Indeed, seven Kastil brothers succeeded in surviving the Spanish expulsion and finally reaching safe haven in Gaza, but the truth is, originally there were eight Kastils, and the story of the eighth brother that we'll introduce here family tradition prefers to keep secret, justly or not.

Most members of the Kastil family in those days resided in the town of Tori De Mormojon, which is in Castilia, or Castalah according to the Arab historians. The oldest son, Yudah, had a flourishing factory for the production of soap made from the lavender plant. Around this factory, which his father founded, or nearby, the members of the seven brothers' families, some of whom dealt with the cultivation of the relentless purple plants' broad fields, also comfortably made a living. The others raised their flocks and shepherded them, in particular Moreno sheep. Their wives worked at combing wool, or producing fabric.

Immediately after King Fernando the Second and his wife

Queen Isabella announced the edict determining that the Jews must convert to Catholicism, or leave Castilia and Aragon within four months, the oldest brother, Yudah, sent his daughter Esther to convene the family members for an urgent, secret nighttime meeting. It was a very cold night. The family members arrived from all sides of Tori De Mormojon, and their breath was visible for a moment and immediately disappeared.

Almost forty people arrived. People who stayed with one another on Shabbat and holidays, and visited each other during the time of mourning, though they hadn't experienced an urgent, secret gathering like this before. Yudah spoke slowly in a broken voice and said he foresees the future, and that he doesn't believe Don Yitzhak Abarbanel, Fernando and Isabella's treasurer, will be able to convince them to cancel the evil decree, at the most he'd obtain some sort of extension, and what's the point of postponing the end?

He came to the meeting after already making up his mind: they must leave immediately, and without wasting the time still remaining to them. They must flee for their lives before all the Jews are banging on the exit doors and due to too much crowding and panic one won't know what to do next. The brothers believed that if their successful older brother, the one proud of the family soap factory and his expertise, and whose soul was so attached to Tori De Mormojon and the purple lavender fields—if their brother determined that they must escape, there was no doubting him. It is clear that no one from among the Kastil brothers and their family members considered the possibility of converting.

Yudah gave them twenty days for preparation, and also arranged for their rabbi, Rabbi Yitzhak Avohav, to join them and along with him a good many of his followers.

The Kastils decided to move to nearby Portugal and to put down roots among its Jews. At first they would settle there quietly, and afterwards would try to buy fields and again establish the lavender soap factory. The faster they left, the higher the prices they would obtain in exchange for their possession, and they would take some provisions, fabrics, and of course gold rings.

It was decided that Sarah, Yudah's wife, would sew for them handbags tied to their bodies—for everyone, down to the last infant. For those she'd embroider chicks on the handbag, she thought to herself, so they'd know that they came from a home where there was plenty, and that they were loved there as well.

She sensed that from the moment they left Tori Da Mormojon—that there was no knowing what would happen to them. And indeed she acted wisely and with foresight. And as for the adults—more than once it happened that a Kastil emptied the cloth handbag of another Kastil, the same handbag that Sarah sewed for him, a minute after the other returned his soul to the Creator.

The Kastils therefore left equipped with all that one could take—first north, and afterwards west, to Portugal. They joined other groups of Jews who thought that Portugal was the solution. Only soon it became clear to them that they were naïve and that the idea of blending with the Jewish community in Portugal was a bitter illusion. The Portuguese had their own Jews, and were not in need of more "ill-tempered." The Kastils fleeing for their lives were amazed by their dismissive attitudes. They didn't at all notice it wasn't a horde that had reached them, but rather honorable Jews, one of whom even possessed the knowledge of how to produce hard soap, among the best throughout the Iberian Peninsula.

They saw in them excess baggage, outcast refugees who were to be isolated, and they erected camps for them with poor living conditions. Many of them died from epidemics, among them the rabbi Yitzhak Abuhav. Sarah too almost died in the refugee camp, but she survived. Also her husband and three children: the twins Nissim and Natan, and Esther the first-born, they got sick and recovered.

Not many days later the authorities in Portugal surrendered

to the inhabitants' pressure and put the refugees who had survived onto twenty-five large ships, in order to transport them as far away as possible.

The chronicles tell of hair-raising stories. Some of the ships had cruel captains, who dropped Jews off in North African deserts and remote islands in the Mediterranean Sea, and didn't heed their pleas to be returned to the ship. Women and children were kidnapped, dispersed, and sold as servants and slaves.

A ship full of Jews rife with hardship and thin as skeletons arrived in the city of Malaga. Among them was the family of Yudah and Sarah. Jews, of course, couldn't go onshore, unless they converted. Day after day a priest would come onto the ship and ask the travelers if they were now ready to make the sign of the cross. It was an endless nightmare. A hungry, tormented person says no-no-no, but eventually says, "yes." The ship's captain came to Yudah and Sarah with an offer they couldn't refuse: they would sell him their daughter Esther—in exchange for an amount that was neither a lot nor a little. The offer was the lesser of two evils, because they didn't touch the twins Nissim and Natan. They agreed out of great despair, and with the encouragement of Esther herself. Esther went to her fate without making any noise. And soon she was sold onward, for a higher price, after she was healthy and attractive as well.

A day after Sarah was forced to say goodbye to her daughter, all her hair lost its color in a single night, and in the morning she saw that deep lines of sadness furrowed the length of her face. Yudah told her that their daughter was holy and sacrificed herself for the sake of her family, a deed equivalent to a martyr's death, but Sarah found in this no consolation.

Two days later the parents and the twins surrendered and converted to Christianity. And then they returned to beloved Tori Da Mormojon and managed to buy back a significant portion of their possession, and more than a bit of this was made possible thanks to the funds from selling Esther.

The town's priest, Onoretto De Mendosa, received the

lost sons with a warm welcome, a deed that was not consistent with the spirit of the time or the underlying messages of the Inquisition. De Mendosa was enlightened and patient toward the Marranos, since he understood that Rome wasn't built in a day. He demanded from them their presence at church for Sunday Mass, and insisted they perform the rituals, but he did not enter their homes to check the true extent of their conversion. He assumed that the process would last a generation if they were hard on them, and two generations at the most, if they let them live their lives peacefully. Therefore there was no point making their lives miserable.

De Mendosa also assisted the family extensively in the negotiations to reclaim the factory and the fields. The price they now paid was higher but only a bit more than they once received. A widow named Bonita and her five children had taken over the spacious house, and this Bonita was willing to leave it only after the priest promised her a bright future both after death and in the short term as well.

Yudah wanted to put the twins to work in the soap factory, but Sarah refused, and wanted them to stay with her at home all the time, because she was afraid to be alone. This fear was something new, and began only after they returned to the town.

One day she told the priest De Mendosa, during the sacrament of confession, about what had occurred with their daughter Esther, and about the terrible guilt she felt.

"At home," Sarah told him without seeing his face, "her name is not mentioned, we even changed her room entirely. We are silent, but my husband is no longer who he once was, and I myself am unable to remain home alone and am ruining Diego and Pedro's lives. I know that because of what I did with Esther I will go to Hell. Even as a Jewess I would have gone to Hell."

Diego and Pedro were the new names of the twins Nissim and Natan—but not within the home.

"You saved your entire family from Hell," De Mendosa said to her.

"At night I dream that she returns," she said and choked up

and began weeping at length, and the weeping granted De Mendosa time to think. He said to her:

"Do you promise that if Esther returns you will perform all the sacraments beyond that which is required?"

"What do you mean? Without any doubt. I promise that I will go above and beyond what is required," she said. "I will be the model Converso in all of Castilia," she declared and promised.

"I will check what is in my power to do," De Mendosa said.

Sarah didn't know if he was making a guarantee or merely speaking with good intentions to calm her. But the good-hearted De Mendosa worked his connections in the church and the Benedictine monasteries, in one of which he spent his youth, and did not let the matter rest.

For some time already he had wanted to hold a celebratory Mass in honor of something, which would prove who runs thing in this town, and he assumed that returning Esther would be a suitable event and also an opportunity for the townsfolk to atone for their treatment of the Conversos. The return of the daughter to the father and mother, the new Christians, who had lost all trace of her, could be a high point in the life of the community, a miracle that would instill pure Christian faith in all those who had lost their way.

Eventually Esther was found safe and sound on a tiny island called "the Island of Tarifa," the southernmost tip of Europe, between the Rock of Gibraltar and North Africa. The Spanish encouraged settlement there, as a shield against enemy invasions from North Africa, whereas the Church provided an incentive to all who settled in the Island of Tarifa for at least a year: retroactive pardon as well as forgiveness in advance.

Captain Juan Lopez, Esther said, sold her, on the very day he bought her, to a Basque by the name of Francisco Malyado, who was waiting on shore. Esther, who was designated as a slave, was impregnated by him and fled, and in her escape miscarried the baby. He hunted her down and retrieved her, but she was very ill after the miscarriage. So Malyado sent her to his sister Elvira on the Island of Tarifa. Heronimo, the sister's deaf and dumb husband, was the lighthouse keeper there.

In Tarifa Esther was brought into the bosom of Christianity for the second time. She slowly recovered with the assistance of the good-intentioned Elvira, and also learned from her how to raise Iberian pigs, what they eat, and how curious and smart they are. Elvira also taught her their body language, and how to train the pig, by means of the proper stick, to always be to the right of the stick and never sway from the path. And in general, Elvira got her back on her feet and taught her many things, about both life and pigs as well.

Heronimo did not disturb Esther's sleep at night, and the three of them lived peacefully in the lighthouse. In truth, Esther concluded to everyone's amazement, this was the loveliest period of her life. She said that Elvira understood when she avoided taking care of the pigs on Shabbat.

Esther recommended to her family members that they raise a herd of Iberian pigs in Tori De Mormojon. Because not only would this be exceedingly lucrative, but it would also prove to everyone that their conversion was complete, and there would be no need to explain to anyone why they cleaned themselves and their house on Friday, or separated the thigh tendon from the meat.

"If we have a herd like this, mother," Esther turned to Sarah, who was paralyzed by the new onslaught of facts and their impact on her and her life, "no one will dare bother us. Trust me. I learned a lot with Elvira, and I can take care of pigs like that, on the condition that you make me a pen."

"So we'll need to set aside a plot of land from one of the lavender fields," Diego-Nissim said.

"With the money we earn from the pigs we'll be able to buy more lavender fields!" Esther said assertively.

Sarah followed Yudah's deep silence with concern.

"I think that this is an excellent idea," said Pedro-Natan.

"Me too," Diego-Nassin echoed.

"The males are more valuable than the females, but don't worry," Esther offered more of her knowledge, perhaps too soon, "the pigs reproduce quickly. A female that has finished suckling can get pregnant again after a few days. The stronger piglets shove the weaklings to the mother-pig's most distant nipples, which usually don't provide much, and soon they simply die from hunger. But it's possible to locate the weak piglets in time, before they die a natural death, and sell them. Their meat is a rare delicacy among the wealthy."

"I, of course," she quickly added, "didn't eat any pork. I ate only vegetables, and a lot of bread. The bread that they bake there, in Tarifa, is a bit like Passover matzo, only thicker."

Silence fell over the house of the Conversos. Even Esther felt she had spoken too much, but despite this added:

"The pigs are very disciplined animals. They are also strong and don't catch diseases. They are smart and amusing animals."

"And what do they eat?" Yudah asked. Finally he broke his silence, his eyes red with fury.

"Everything," Esther said. "Trees, shrubs, meat, everything."

"Lavender too?" Yudah asked and it appeared that in a moment he would strike his daughter.

"No, don't worry, Father. The lavender would be bitter for the pigs. I know how to control them and can take them to graze far from the house and return them, just to be safe, only after they're full."

Yudah shook his head no to the left and the right, but Sarah of all people was actually pleased. Jewish or Christian—all her children are with her, and alive. It was all for the best. Esther had also learned a trade during her absence, and this trade was an excellent guarantee of their non-Jewishness. It seemed to her, to Sarah, that the worst was already behind her, and that now she must prepare for a new life. This coming Sunday the festive Mass would be held, and Esther would also be baptized for the third time since her abduction.

The priest De Mendosa wanted to change her name from Esther to Maria, but Sarah begged him that her name be switched to Beatrice, a name that was acceptable among Conversos as well. After the ceremony she told De Mendosa about their plans to expand and set up a pigpen, and he advised her to buy relatively thin pigs at the market and to fatten them up. It would be profitable. Thus they could buy more pigs for the same amount of money.

The work of setting up the pen, including the fence, lasted three days—days Yudah spent fasting and mourning. Sarah promised him that they'd no longer go to Mass, except once a month, and that the important Mass was already behind them. "I promise you that I won't touch those impure animals," she said suddenly, "do you believe me?"

And since then, each day, Esther-Beatrice would go out to graze the pigs as far as possible from the house, and would return before dusk, and would care for them then as well, and they on their part gained weight and multiplied.

But then something fell upon the house of the Conversos. Yudah could no longer stand the presence of his daughter Beatrice, because of the terrible smell of pigs that clung to her clothes. In vain the mother scrubbed the daughter's body with the family's lavender soap. In vain she sprinkled her with rose water. A moment after Yudah would meet his daughter, he would always make a movement deep in his guts, as if he were about to vomit, and his body produced the harsh sounds of someone devastated.

Eventually, having no choice, Diego and Pedro built a shack for her, which shared only one wall with the house, and a relatively convenient path ran from it to the pen—so she'd live there, sleep there, eat outside and care for the pigs, take them grazing and slaughter them.

But Yudah sunk entirely into his melancholy and began to avoid going to the soap factory. Very slowly the income from the pigpen became the main income of the family, which got richer and richer from the cursed money of the ostracized daughter. Even Sarah, who in the meantime changed her name to Constansa, kept far away from Esther-Beatrice, whose existence was in fact difficult to forget, since the smell of the pigs clung to the walls of the house and furniture as well, and Sarah could not get rid of it.

This was a terrible period in the history of the family, and it's clear why they prefer to forget it. But the heavens looked out for them so that the angel De Mendosa would be by their side. Such a good-hearted priest, at a time when in other places the Inquisition was running wild! In one consultation with De Mendosa, in the face of Yudah's indifference, Sarah-Constansa was able to rent the soap factory and the fields of flowers to a close friend of the priest, who employed nuns from the nearby monastery as workers.

In those times most of the information people had reached them by rumor, and after the great expulsion the Jews' abandoned cemeteries were a source of many strange rumors. One of the rumors was that the vegetation that grows around the Jewish tombstones is especially excellent for the health and strength of pigs, and nourishes them better than regular grazing. And indeed, many pig shepherds allowed their pigs to set upon Jewish cemeteries, and sometimes a pig would sprawl out and rest on a tombstone. In contrast to this, Esther always avoided bringing her pigs to the Jewish cemetery so they could taste its abundance, and once three youths saw Esther kicking three pigs angrily, until she nearly cracked their heads, while shouting at them to no longer even go close to a Jewish cemetery, and these youths were quick to inform on her until finally the cat was out of the bag.

So it happened that Esther of all people brought the Inquisition to Tori Da Mormochon. True the rumor reached the ears of other informers that the A-Rachel family was providing kosher meat to the Conversos in town, and Constansa-Sarah was spotted returning on a Thursday from the house of the A-Rachel family and in her hand was a wrapped package that was not in her hand when she went there, and another time they saw her hanging up sheets early on Friday morning and said that she was doing this so that they'd manage to dry before the arrival of the Sabbath—this meant that the eye of the Inquisition was on the mother and not just the daughter, but the volunteer gentry, who arrested heretics in service of the Inquisition, preferred to imprison the young, sturdy daughter, as it was preferable to deal with her first before she had offspring.

In vain the mother Sarah cried out for them to take her instead, and Yudah caught and held his wife as she fell and lost consciousness. The priest Da Mendosa heard wailing from the house of the Conversos, but what could he do? However in the middle of the night Constansa knocked on the door of his house and asked him if there weren't some way in which he could help her as he had helped them in the past. Perhaps he has some connections with the Inquisition, she wondered repeatedly in all sorts of ways. The priest answered in the negative about the matter of connections, but he recommended to her the advocate known as Juan Da Hosis to represent the pig shepherdess before the Inquisition.

Diego and Pedro hurried to sell the pigs, so that they wouldn't be confiscated, as was customary then, for the need of funding Esther's imprisonment. Yudah generously accepted the selling of the pigs. And in general, he suddenly came back to life and discovered new strengths. He returned to the factory, released the nuns and brought back his past workers, and reached an agreement with the monastery to divide profits into equal portions. The color returned to his cheeks. He looked ten years younger.

Sarah was not pleased by the recovery of her husband, who opposed hiring the advocate, who indeed charged dearly. Eventually Yudah conceded, because he couldn't resist his wife's argumentativeness.

Da Hosis was a converted Jew himself, and was familiar with

the weak points of the Inquisition trial. He was about thirty-five years old, a gaunt and feeble man, whose cheeks were sunken in as if his days were numbered. He tried to use in Esther's favor the period she spent in Tarifa. She was there for over a year and was thus entitled to the bonus of complete absolution. But the prosecuting inquisitor argued against him that he had no proof that the accused lived in Tarifa as a Christian, after all she was baptized only upon her return to Tori Da Mormochon. In vain Esther repeated that she had already been baptized in Tarifa for the second time, that she was in fact baptized in Malaga. They didn't believe her.

Da Hosis therefore sent someone to search for Elvira, wife of Heronimo, in order to testify for her, but the emissary returned empty-handed: neither Elvira nor Heronimo were located on the Island of Tarifa. After despairing of this direction the advocate argued with complete confidence that no Jew committed to the Jewish faith would touch a pig, let alone deal with multiple pigs, and he contorted his face with much disgust, because he himself was revolted by this trade.

Only Esther, when they tortured her, admitted heresy. And it was true that a confession during torture was not considered valid, and it was necessary for the accused to repeat it with a clear mind and not in the torture chamber, but Esther again confessed in a calm atmosphere as well. Sitting opposite the Inquisitor she signed the confession out of "free will and clear mind."

The investigation and trial lasted two years, and finally it was decided that it was upon Esther to become reconciled with the Church, that is, to return to the bosom of Christianity and to wear for a year the penitential garment, the Sanbenito. At first she would wear it in the auto-da-fé procession, and afterward for half a year in which she would stay with a reliable Christian family in a sort of house arrest (the Inquisition was always short on prisons, and it was forced to settle for a stay like this of its condemned with a family), and in the end for another half year in her town. After a year the Sanbenito would be hung up in her town's church, and would always remain hanging there, as a mark of her and her family's disgrace, as long as she lived.

The Sanbenito was a kind of yellow caftan, which reached down to the knees, and on it were painted dragons and demons and flames of hell, and if the flames faced downward, this meant that the convict would not be burned alive but would instead choke first. However a Sanbenito like that was for those sentenced to be burned, whereas Esther-Beatrice's Sanbenito, as someone who had repented and confessed, was simpler. It was a stiff, yellow tunic, upon which was painted a red cross in front and in back, and an inseparable part of it was a ridiculous, pointed conical cap, from the same woven fabric, which was visible at a distance.

After six months in the house of Christians with roots in a nearby town, Beatrice returned home. Her two brothers had already re-established the pigpen business and had become the owners of the herd—she herself was now forbidden from owning a herd, or even making soap—but the stench didn't cling to the brothers, because they managed the herd from a distance—they hired Christians who did the work instead of them.

The day when Esther returned from exile with the pointed cap on her small head would never be forgotten in the family. This was a day blacker than black. They never knew shame like this, and they didn't know what to do with themselves. Everyone found a way to avoid Beatrice. The brothers announced that if she didn't move immediately to the shack they built for her in the past, they'd leave. Her mother Sarah hardened her heart as well and demanded that her daughter maintain a distance of at least fifty paces from her, as if everyone didn't know that they were mother and daughter. And Yudah—Yudah kept quiet as was his way, didn't speak a word to his daughter, good or bad.

Pedro and Diego also went wild with rage when it became clear to them that in another half year the penitential garment would forever hang in the town church, as long as their sister was alive, and that they'd have to confront the caftan every Sunday, a thing that would also make it impossible for them to find a Christian bride. In vain they attempted to convince De Mendosa—he didn't have much patience for them, he closed the door in their faces, and since then the twins walked about with a ghostly expression on their faces.

Esther again became the shepherd of the family's pigs and was careful to maintain the distance that they demanded of her. Day after day she dealt with the difficulty of walking with the caftan and the conical cap when going out to the pasture as well. If only there weren't that cap, Sarah-Constansa thought as she gazed at her daughter returning with the pigs. In Tori De Mormochon they would see her pointed cap from a distance and announce her arrival and plug up their noses.

As a good Christian Sarah-Constansa severed all her ties to other Conversos in those days, and also went again and again to confess to De Mendosa about her feelings of guilt. She still rose earlier than usual on Fridays and undertook a thorough cleaning, and on Shabbat would dress up nice, as she dressed on the Christians' holidays.

Esther, who understood well the feelings of her family members, would take the pigs to grazing places further and further away, and sometimes would return to her shack only after a day or two, and thus when she was once late to return, even after a week no one asked any questions. They didn't search for her, and they didn't look forward expectantly to her return. De Mendosa said to Sarah that in the end this was a blessing for the whole family, because now the caftan wouldn't hang in the church. De Mendosa also said to Constanza, that if she and the rest of her family behaved properly, the Inquisition would let them be from now on. Thus Sarah didn't say a word to anyone when she washed the sons' bloodstained clothes.

Two months later a neighbor brought them the Sanbenito garment, which he found in a forest torn, stained, and rotting. That same day Pedro and Diego made a bonfire and completely burned the Sanbenito, and the next day the empty pigpen went up in flames. As for the pigs that were with Esther—those scattered in every direction throughout the Iberian Peninsula and joined wild herds, which would run through the streets of the larger cities.

Chapter 9
The Counter Girl Gets Leverage

The counter girl at the Yellow convenience store, the one in the Rokach Gardens gas station, didn't look as she had before. Usually her gaze was deep and focused, and she would provide the customer with the item they requested while closed up inside herself. But on this day, almost at noon of a very hot day in the month of September, at a time when there was stress at the counter, the gaze of the counter girl was weak and glazed over, and even towards the Older Daughter, who would sometimes talk with her about this and that, she now slung a pair of forlorn, inquisitive eyes, and her lips were sealed.

The Older Daughter got it: someone broke the counter girl's heart, and she's barely keeping it together on her shift. She merely hears what the customers want and acts as swiftly as possible, in order to get rid of them, but they don't decrease, instead they multiply more and more—because there's an exhibition at the Exhibition Gardens and crowds are flocking here from all corners of the country's center.

The Older Daughter's attitude about the black-eyed counter girl from the roadside convenience store was special for a few reasons. First, she was the same age as the Older Daughter's Older Daughter. Second, her cappuccino was excellent, and only from her could you get good coffee in the vicinity of Rokach at three in the morning. Third, she wanted to be infected by her diligence. Oshrat worked night after night, and sometimes night after morning after night, almost without any breaks.

The Older Daughter would leave her good tips, as if she were thus buying her attention. And then, without being asked, and after she had succeeded in getting her to talk, she began to give her advice. For instance, don't leave ten *agurah* coins in the stainless steel bowl for tips, because they cause additional people to leave ten *agurah* tips. One copies the other. That way she'll never be able to save and quit her difficult daily routine. The Older Daughter advised Oshrat to immediately collect the ten *agurah* coins and hide them, and even get rid of the half-shekel ones, and to leave only shekels in the bowl—two shekels and five shekels, and actually, leave only silver coins—so people will copy each other.

The counter girl's black eyes usually sparkled, and she had black hair that grew under a baseball cap she barely ever removed.

She had somewhat prominent teeth. She never spoke about her past, her home, or her plans for the future, but you could see in her that she didn't want to end her life behind counters.

Many times it would happen that guys whose night out ended too early came and sat down on the other side of the counter and tried to get Oshrat to talk, to tell them her story and flirt with them. She would get embarrassed and laugh, as if she were learning the ways of the world too late, and was only good at the placement of her hat on her head.

That being the case, she was tough with them, and the guys, who were sometimes drunk after going out, more than once asked for the Older Daughter's help, for her to help them and convince her to accede and agree to speak with them.

The Older Daughter always sung the praises of the counter girl, but said that she was free to do as she wanted. More than once the guys' eyes lit up at the sound of the Older Daughter's exaggerated descriptions of the counter girl's great spirit and courage, if she would just finally notice that they were listening to her. These descriptions were over the top and full of highfalutin bombast, but were challenging to those listening to her.

And now, so it appeared, she had come to accept one of them, and a broken heart was the result.

The Older Daughter didn't know what to do (there was nothing to do, nothing to be done), and left there with her coffee in a disposable cup. Did she have a part in the counter girl's agitation and pain? Is she guilty of the counter girl's abandonment into a world without innocence?

A day later, late at night, almost at dawn, she again came there to drink coffee and buy some item she had run out of at home. Oshrat wasn't there. At the end of the counter, on its other side, sat an Ethiopian gas station attendant by the name of Demasalal, who was surfing on a laptop, and behind the counter was a regular Israeli, mixed, a son of native Israeli parents, without any immigrant complex. His hands moved confidently, and he was at one with his existence and managed everything fearlessly.

"Where's Oshrat?" the Older Daughter asked.

"She's not here."

"Is she supposed to come?"

"Don't know. What's it to you?"

A large van noisily approached.

"The newspapers arrived," called out the Israeli lacking the immigrant complex, and Demasalal arranged small round plastic tables in lines perpendicular to the counter.

It was Friday, before morning, and on Friday all the papers are heavy due to so many supplements.

The next day, on Saturday morning, the Older Daughter stopped at the gas station specifically to check if Oshrat had arrived at work, and she found that she had indeed arrived and was standing there, but she was busy with a customer then and didn't take her eyes away from him at all, and she couldn't guess what her eyes were saying.

The customer explained something to her at length. The Older Daughter waited patiently until he finished, and when he finished, and she was finally able to meet the counter girl's gaze, the Older Daughter smiled and said hello.

Oshrat barely answered her, and a barrier to the outside was reflected in her eyes.

It already was clear now that one of the suitors had made his way to her, and she had responded and given in to him.

She was confused, but not dazed like on Wednesday, when the masses assembled at the counter. The focus had in fact returned to her black eyes, but it was an offhanded focus, like she was only doing the minimum, as if from here on out she already understood the world, and this would be the prescription in her gaze's focus: only in order to see. Nothing more needed.

Now she even avoided the gaze of the Older Daughter, who was sad to find disappointment in her eyes, and a tiny, first speck of bitterness. Oshrat had not reached the heights. The Older Daughter sighed for her, and said something she hoped would draw the counter girl's attention, but in vain.

She wanted Oshrat to smile. This was very important for human morale.

But Oshrat didn't smile.

Eventually she did her a favor—or having no choice placed both eyes upon her—and asked her as if the Older Daughter had been absent from the convenience mart for months:

"A cappuccino for you?"

"No," the Older Daughter said and grabbed some mints. "Just this."

Erev Rosh Hashanah 2009 arrived, with the heavy traffic at the required pre-meal time.

The Older Daughter needed to pick up her mother Vivienne, and her aunt Adele and uncle Vita, who were unable to find an available cab at the required time.

Everyone went to Ramat Aviv, to Amatsia, the Only Daughter's widower, as he and his two daughters, Levona and Timna, hosted everyone for the holiday meal, and they ordered all the food from the store Mizr'ah.

On her way to do the picking up she stopped at the

convenience store, and look, the counter girl is there on her shift, not taking part in any holiday meal, not at her own place, not at the head of her family, and not with a man's family. The Older Daughter went over to her. Oshrat lifted up her head, looked at her, and smiled.

There was relief in the heart of the Older Daughter.

"I just wanted to say *shanah tovah*," she said, and the counter girl nodded and smiled some more.

The damage has been reduced somehow, thanks perhaps to some other consolation, or thanks to the time that has passed, the Older Daughter said to herself and drove to Bavli to pick up her mother and Vivienne, and to Yehudah Hamaccabi Street to pick up Vita and Adele. Her son and daughter were with their father this year.

The Older Daughter's old Hyundai Getz was not clean or tidied up as is proper before an event as festive as the Rosh Hashanah meal, and everyone crowded into the white car in tacit agreement, next to newspapers yellowed from the sun, and next to empty juice bottles, and next to the heavy folders, spreading dust, of old income tax documents from various years. Eight months had already passed since the accountant gave them to the Older Daughter to keep at home, and they're still in the car.

The car was totally beaten up and also missing half a bumper, but its engine was very powerful. The Older Daughter started driving to Ramat Aviv. She felt great shame that her car appeared so neglected, as if she lived inside it. She peeked at the others through the mirror. They looked as if they were coming to terms with their fate, and the thing gave her comfort for a few moments.

Immediately after they crossed Weizmann Street a cab passed by them and Vivienne said:

"Here's a cab!"

A bit before they merged onto Namir Way another cab passed.

"Here's another cab," Vivienne said.

"And here's another cab," she said again.

On Namir Way another two cabs were counted and a great distress penetrated the white Hyundai, the passengers of which are trying to reach the Rosh Hashanah meal despite all the difficult memories and intra-family conflicts.

"I swear to you, Vivienne," Adele said in her trembling voice of recent years, since the death of her Only Daughter, "I sat with the phone for an hour and I called all the stations in the area . . . they told me there were none, no cabs."

"And here's a cab—" Vivienne kept going.

"Mom, stop," the Older Daughter said.

"—a completely empty cab . . ."

"That's the first round that's done," the Older Daughter explained to everyone sitting in the car, "they dropped off the passengers and now they're going to do the next round."

Adele's face was miserable. She didn't see Vita's face, because she had to drive and look forward. But in recent months Uncle Vita's eyes grew more and more cloudy, and the difference between the white of the eye and the cornea was as if subject to negotiation.

"Here's a seventh cab," Vivienne said. "Those are definitely people who didn't remember at the last moment, but instead ordered a cab at noon," she added as if amazed at the way of the world.

The next day, when the Older Daughter asked her mother why she made Adele's life miserable like that with matter of the cab, Vivienne countered:

"And what do you think Adele said about you? 'Why did she only go into the bathroom now? She had all day to shower. She knew there's a meal this evening, so why does she remember to shower only now?' How am I going to keep quiet about that? If that was *your* daughter, would you keep quiet?"

"Sorry, sorry," the Older Daughter hurried to apologize.

At the end of the holiday the Older Daughter stopped by the convenience store again, and Oshrat the counter girl was there again, and it already seemed that she lived there, behind the merchandise. Her hair was wet like after a shower, but perhaps that was because of hair gel? The hat was resting on the wet hair. It was clear she preferred the store to home.

The Older Daughter asked for a cappuccino and looked at the tip bowl. In it were silver coins of a shekel, and of two shekels, and five, and ten. No more ten-*agurah* coins or half-shekel coins at the most. The Older Daughter left five shekels and was pleased: the counter girl is starting to save money in preparation for something. The counter girl is using the tip bowl like a lever, she has plans for the future.

After many months, who knows how many, the Older Daughter stopped by the convenience store at four in the morning. Under the black hat Oshrat had a very neat bob hairdo, and her self-confidence was tremendous. She handed out instructions to the workers unpacking merchandise before the morning clientele arrived.

"Where'd you disappear to?" she asked the Older Daughter.

"I disappeared?" the Older Daughter reflected. "Right, I disappeared."

"It's been a year," Oshrat said.

"A year?"

A conversation unfolded between the two, and it turned out that the counter girl was starting to study at the Wingate Institute in another two months—towards a certificate as a fitness instructor.

A few years passed, or perhaps just two, and the counter girl completed her studies with honors, yet still continued to work nights at the convenience store, albeit only on weekends and holidays.

One day it appeared she fell wrong, maybe on some pole vault jump, because for two months she had an elastic bandage around the base of her hand, but she still continued working on holidays and weekends.

Afterwards it came out that she had an accident on her bike. The Older Daughter did see her one morning peddling quickly, standing up, on her bike—against the direction of traffic, as if there were no laws in the world.

After the accident Oshrat the counter girl was not to be seen in the store, and when the Older Daughter asked about her, they answered that she's recuperating, but there's no one like her. They're giving her time and waiting for her return.

A few months passed, and one night, before dawn, the Older Daughter went to the convenience store to get a cappuccino, even though she had milk and coffee at home. She felt suffocated. The house was getting to her and wanted to bury her beneath it, and she got into the Hyundai, started it up, drove, arrived, entered the gas station and asked for a cappuccino out loud, even though she saw no one behind the counter.

"I hardly work here," Oshrat said as she burst forth from the darkness behind the snack bar with the hat on her head, "just do a shift here and there."

"Did I ask something? I thought you already left. What's with the injury from the accident? Are you okay? Recovered?"

"Almost," she said and served the Older Daughter her first-rate cappuccino. This time the hat was carelessly resting on her head, and her black hair was long, spilling from the hat and spreading over her shoulders.

Chapter 10
Vietnam

It was a warm and very disappointing winter, which came after a series of arid winters, a result of global warming. Rain would fall in torrents for two days, and then a two-week break would come, during which time a heat wave would prevail, but the weathermen were ashamed to say "heat wave," or "*chamsin*," and said, "hot for the season."

No one had ever seen weather like this. Air conditioners. August in the middle of November.

It was late evening. The Older Daughter left almost running from the teachers' lounge of a high school in the suburbs of Tel Aviv, after a lecture she gave there, and hurried home. Two religious women hurried after her. One of them looked like she was about to cry, to the point that she never opened her mouth. The second one said:

"Excuse me, is it true that in one of your books you criticized Chabad? That's what I heard."

The Older Daughter said immediately:

"No. What are you talking about, criticism? The opposite of criticism. The opposite."

"Great," said the talking Chabadnik. "Now I can read your books."

The Older Daughter again felt herself to be transparent. Being a writer was too spiritual an activity for the era.

She wanted to return to her car as fast as possible and to continue on from there. Hurry, she said to herself, rush home, to forgetting, to sleep.

After she got into the car the heavens suddenly opened and

a savage rain began. It pounded hyperbolically on the roof and ricocheted off the front windshield, to the point that she barely saw a thing. Fear gripped her. She felt that the storm was starting to exceed the Israeli dimensions she was used to, and before her was something she had never seen.

She looked at the tops of the palm trees. They had almost been decapitated. A horror show. The wipers weren't working as they should, and the rain fell to earth face-first, as if surrendering to gravity.

The streets were already roaring rivers, which flowed single-mindedly in the direction of the Ayalon stream—the same stream that had been dried up to become the road surrounding Tel Aviv, and now it would surely be flooded. The waters lifted up all the summer's dryness and took it with them onwards, as if into eternity. Stupid that they dried up streams, she thought, and to pave highways of all things. They aggravated nature, and it responded first with dryness, and now with a great storm, with gallons of rain and ear-splitting thunder, which show man just how easily he can be erased.

Little by little the rain scaled down to familiar dimensions. It was even possible to say "blessed rain." Even the drainage worked well now.

The light at the next intersection was working, but was lying on the ground and told its good news to the heavens, because of some accident from before the rain, and this intersection was dangerous for traffic. She waited for calm in the traffic and traveled home. On a still unpaved path she turned left and parked her car as usual, perpendicular to the path.

In the railway building perpendicular to hers they had begun adding sun balconies for all the tenants on the south side (who wouldn't see sun because of the tall trees). There were those who were about to turn the new balcony into an all-purpose room, and one couple was even about to put in an additional kitchen at that height, among the trees. Due to the construction work trucks went up on the lawns and had already created mud puddles from the previous rains. Someone had placed a few tiles to make a temporary path, and she moved from one to the next. By the time she got to her building the rain had managed to soak her entirely, and she swore to herself that no more would she budge without an umbrella and a raincoat. Here the winter has arrived, the deception is over.

The next day the sun came out, and the temperature rose to seventy-seven degrees, and at times even to eighty. Trucks with cement and without cement, and with cranes of this sort and that, drove through the puddles and continued to leave new tire tracks in the mud, and if one looked only at the part of the puddles filled with brown water, and the tire tracks, one might think that this was Vietnam during the war, and not a quiet, rustic neighborhood, where they're merely adding sun balconies on the south side through two entrances, or more correctly quiet balconies among the tall trees. A greater war's violence was on the lawn, relative to the pastorality of the neighborhood, and all for a few balconies—indeed, for tenants with motivation and vigor.

Another dry day passed. The time was almost seven in the morning. All the birds had some time ago already burst forth onto the world in the regular order: the first was a white-breasted kingfisher, which would pierce the silence with a sustained shriek even before the start of sunrise. The sunbirds would wake after it and scatter short, high tweets into the air, and then one could also hear the calls of the crows, which already had command over their living spaces in the neighborhood's treetops and roofs. Sometimes, above all the treetops and homes, seagulls would fly, but wouldn't stop. In the meantime the air filled up with sparrows.

The man who was becoming more and more religious, and

his fresh wife, who was becoming religious as well, who appeared to be on the cusp of forty, returned from the synagogue on the main street. They walked energetically, and accompanied their talking with broad hand gestures.

How lonely this man had been before, the Older Daughter thought while looking at them from her window.

A tolerant *sephardi* man, tall and attractive, wearing the large *kipa* of the newly religious, with Israeli diction, who would ride his bike each morning to synagogue and back again. And on Yom Kippur—what solemnity! And of course, without the bike.

He lived in part of the only private residence in the neighborhood, a house that was in no way a villa, but rather a sort of patchwork estate, structures attached one to the other, some with asbestos roofs, and other with tin roofs. Transit camp housing from days that had passed, which couldn't be vacated because of some law, and in most of it a devoutly religious family had lived for three generations now. They have at least half an acre, and they work it using ancient methods.

The newly religious man rents one of those patches from them.

He would greet her and ask how she was. This was before the first drought, when she still dared to work in the shared garden, before she abandoned it out of fear that the neighbors, who also paid the water bill, would catch her watering the plants and with a hose at that. Since then all the plants had died of thirst.

Only one time did they exchange more than just greetings. He told her that he got divorced from his wife because she didn't want to become religious. She remained with their two children in Kfar-Sabba, and he pays her alimony in accordance with the law. It was clear that if her faith grew stronger, perhaps he would return and there would be something between them, but first she had to get stronger, much stronger.

Now the fresh but not young couple gets closer and closer to her, the increasingly religious man, and his new wife, modest and pious and with a scarf on her head. The meeting takes place in the puddle-ridden, Vietnamese region. The newly religious man and his wife stand hand-in-hand, and everyone grabs a mud-free piece of land.

"Shalom," the neighbor says.

"Shalom."

"How are you?" he asks.

"Good, thanks," and a moment later she adds without being asked: "Mazal tov."

"Ah," the neighbor chuckles, "thank you very much. But how are you?" he appears truly interested.

"Everything's fine," she mumbles and takes care not to fall into Vietnam, and he and his wife turn and walk down the gravel path. He doesn't introduce his new wife to her, who throws a banishing look her way.

But a silence falls between the members of the couple as well. A silence the Older Daughter comprehends without much work. Though soon the conversation between them starts up again; they return to what they were grasping before and continue splitting hairs.

A few days later the Older Daughter passed by the entrance to their home. The newly religious man tilled all the soil there and placed red, triangular stones to mark a plot of land, but the years he spent returning to religion erased in him the basic knowledge that plants need sun, and surely there isn't a drop of sun here. The house and the plot face north, and the organized neighborhood—its trees, its buildings, and their additions—hides their little bit of east. But he planted there and sowed and waited.

This was no longer winter, this scam. If they're turning on sprinklers in January, it's a sign that they've internalized the fact that there's no winter. Despair crawled into the heart of the nation. One man slaughtered an entire family, including a three-month old baby—all out of revenge for the father of the family who fired him. Cruelty like this has not been seen in the country since its establishment. What despair. Would be better to write on a pack of cigarettes that the cigarettes cause despair, and not that the cigarettes cause disease and death. People fear despair more than death. Death doesn't do it for them any longer, despair does. Despair like this has not been seen in the country since its establishment. Here the Older Daughter is splitting hairs, but the newly religious man reads only the scriptures.

They hadn't yet finished building the sun balconies. In other words, a few more months passed. It's lasting forever. All these buildings started out as railway buildings, and over the years they added a substantial northern addition in the shape of a pentagon, and now they're adding a southern addition to them in the shape of a rectangle, and the notion of the train is gradually being forgotten, and a modular building is being created, which perhaps from above, from the atmosphere, has some sort of meaning. For a year already they're adding sun balconies to the building across the way, and the enthusiasm between the fresh couple has subsided as well. They already walk a step apart from each other and remain silent.

Their garden that was supposed to be blooming now at the peak of productivity remained sad and desolate. One might think that the recently religious man's new wife got pregnant and because of this the enthusiasm between them subsided, but that's not how it is. The minimalist winter passed and the new wife is not pregnant. The one whose faith grows stronger goes to synagogue alone like before, but it seems that he has lost the desire for this as well. Before he still had hope. *She* killed his hope. It's impossible to blame her—he too killed something in her. She appears sunken in melancholy. Walks alone in the street, her head covered in a scarf and bent crookedly to one side. She's not content. This is not what she prayed for.

And the apartment owners had yet to begin bursting forth from their houses into the new addition and connecting to it!

They only dug spots for the electricity and ditches for the plumbing, and according to what she saw in other homes, in which they already finished building the additions—they're just calling it a balcony, people are simply adding a room to the apartment, and electric shutters.

If the fresh, sad couple doesn't go to couples therapy before the inhabitants of the one-time railway enter their sun balconies, which the mighty trees cast shadows on, they're liable to be in a bad situation. They'll see the readied sun balconies, get jealous, and their spirits will fall. In couples therapy they'll mitigate the fall and also tell them a bunch of bullshit, but they won't tell them the truth: change apartments. You need sun. There's no sun reaching you. The neighborhood with the trees blocks out the entire east from you!

The woman whose faith is getting stronger suffered from depression due to lack of sun, and he isn't willing to leave the place. He said that their residence here is temporary. Otherwise she wouldn't have entered a ruin like this in her life. Now she understands that she's stuck here. That in general he's tied with family ties to the devout family that owns the apartment, and is helping them hold on to the apartment and the land. He holds tight to the land like an Arab, because the land here is worth millions. The entire structure is still from the days of the transit camps. He housed her in a tiny hut.

It's not a miracle that the woman whose faith is getting stronger isn't becoming pregnant. No sun, no home. And a disappointed soul. A baby has nothing to do here. If she lets him crawl on the grass among the secular women of the neighborhood—they look at her askance, why she doesn't pay to water the lawn, and she herself has a dirt path for the baby. The woman whose faith is getting stronger won't bring a baby to a place like this. They deceived her when they did the matchmaking. They said a divorced man, whose faith is getting stronger, handsome. Not bald, not fat, sitting on land worth millions, and she—a pure virgin, thirty-two years old and not attractive—she consented immediately.

Chapter 11
A Relative's Death

When you're by the deathbed of an eighty-something-year-old man, in the emergency room at Ichilov Hospital, and he's already been anesthetized and placed on a respirator and connected to every possible machine and tube, and above him, behind a rectangular glass with thin strips of metal, a very strong white fluorescent light is on—don't you dare ask the staff to turn off that strong light falling on the face of the dying man. That's their work light!

If you ask, they'll say: "And how will we work?"

But he's already dying, what is there to work on here? That light is cruel. A light like this is poured onto Mordechai Vanunu twenty-four hours a day because he revealed Israel's atomic secrets! This man didn't reveal many secrets, the opposite is true. Usually he kept quiet.

"Doctor, what did he do? He's from among the builders of the country, one of the greats! There almost aren't any like that anymore. He was one of those who paved roads. Dug the soil with his own hands, plowed and planted, and drove this and that kind of tractor. Managed seventeen branches of Bank Discount over the years—and remained a fair and honest man."

Now one could also mention the dying man by name in order to show that he's flesh and blood from the *yishuv*. Perhaps if the doctor hears a first and last name she'll soften up.

But there's nothing to argue about. There's a complete medical staff here already, and they have the upper hand. They're closed off now with the dying man behind a moveable curtain, and they're giving him a wide range of antibiotics instead of leaving him alone. Isn't he finished—what are they doing?

But they can't do otherwise. They took the Hippocratic Oath and they have no choice and no escape. And you thank God that the doctor with the long hair of uneven length, burnt at the ends, hair that hasn't seen a salon for some time now, fell into your lap; a bit chubby in the upper part of the body, with a relatively precise line of eyeliner over the eyelid. Thank God that this isn't the surgeon with the eyeliner above and below the eye, because she's really not worth bothering with. She's a professional and does her job, and she's very busy. And justly so.

This surgeon has a high ponytail as well, elevated and wrapped around itself, and she collects only that half-bun in the surgeon's green cap, and the rest of the taut hair remains out.

The surgeon with the green ponytail is a tall woman with a sculpted figure, in contrast to the pelvis of the one from the ER, which has already swelled up a fair amount, into the dimensions of a barrel really, and her face is quite bloated.

If the one with the barrel-like pelvis is her lot, she must take it down a notch and obtain the maximum possible for the dying. She has a very short fuse, this doctor. If you cross some thin line with her, it can be lit and she'll call for security to throw you out, as if you misbehaved and shook the mattresses. Maybe she lacked a mother's love during her childhood, and maybe she's simply broken. In any case, she's also capable of asking suddenly:

"You tell me that he's your uncle, but how am I to know at all that you're this man's relative?"

Here you must stop on the spot and look straight into her eyes, but under no circumstances say to her: "You're right. I came in off the street and grabbed a random dying man to cry over." You must show restraint and take out ID and show her the last name that the dying man has as well, and not change your expression. You could take a peek at the dying man and to the extent possible copy his expression.

Please, friends! Let her close herself off with the dying man for ten minutes behind the curtain and shoot him up with whatever she wants. He's unconscious. He won't feel anything regardless.

An important recommendation: under no circumstances are you to mutter angrily through the curtain something like: "Finally, after all these years, you're alone with some man behind a curtain."

Let her then be alone for a few minutes with your dying one. Remember that it is within her power to toss you out of the emergency room, and outside there are only the homeless, drunks, and other people.

You do indeed yearn to be with him in his final moments, to speak to him with special tenderness, like to a baby who sprouts up suddenly, and to sing all the songs to him, until death—but here you are being asked again to leave the curtained-off area.

The doctors gather now for a consultation behind the curtain, next to the patient.

Why must the consultations be next to the sick man? Why is it impossible to speak a few meters away from him? After all he's obviously not listening and can't contribute to the conversation.

It's customary. And now we want to confer among ourselves about the patient, and the curtain is to protect us. Please don't interrupt.

Elbows and shoulders stick out through the curtain, and here and there the movement of a head is apparent. They're speaking. Impossible to understand. From time to time they accompany their speech with hand movements and the curtain sways.

Firm in their opinions they move the curtain aside and come out. Did they find a miracle drug? Definitely not. In one consultation it was decided to move him to the internal medicine ward, and all this on the run, with all the tubes and machines.

As a family member of the dying man the very fact of leaving the ER and moving to Internal Medicine encourages you. Maybe there's a chance.

Three head out, running to Internal Medicine with the patient connected to tubes and two monitors he was hooked up to in the ER. They have to go from the basement to the second floor. They start the run from the elevator at the end of emergency surgery. The run is accompanied by a doctor in her six month of pregnancy, and also a nurse. At certain moments perhaps they run at a speed of 5 mph. By the entrance to the elevator the pregnant doctor says to you that there's no room in the elevator and they disappear behind the closing door. But where is the other elevator? You press and press—it doesn't arrive, and thus you've lost them and the dying man who you insist on accompanying.

It may be that while you're looking for them, after you finally reached the second floor, that they too suddenly burst forth from some elevator. Fine, they got mixed up and lost their way in the architectural labyrinth of the patchwork hospital, and now everyone as a single person enters Internal Medicine, the door of which opens on its own before them.

Running after the runners was good for you. For some time you haven't run. It hurled a healthy concoction into your brain and improved your mood despite the awful and terrible situation.

At Internal Medicine G they bring the one-time kibbutz member into the department's ICU and tell you to wait outside. They connect him to all the stationary machines that exist in the place on a permanent basis, and remove the mobile units, in order to return them to the ER in the basement.

"In the meantime get some coffee," they say to you. But there's no coffee, because today's Saturday, and you have to walk to Aroma Café outside the hospital, and it's such a pain.

When you return from Aroma after the whole walk, the new Internal Medicine staff won't let you into the ICU at all. So what came of the whole "in the meantime get some coffee"? What came was that they put you farther away from the one-time kibbutz member, and you're beside yourself with helplessness. Look, it appears that a young, blue-eyed doctor has come out to assist you, but he says to you with kind eyes that he's sorry. They did everything, with all the technology at their disposal, but unfortunately the man died. Are you interested in seeing him? While you were at Aroma and waiting in the long line—he passed away. But regardless you weren't allowed to get near to him, nor could you have prevented his death. After all, this is why he arrived at the ER.

All of a sudden the entire department transforms. A geyser of consideration for the one-time kibbutz member, who just now died, erupts, and for his relatives too. Now they allow anyone who wants to go in "to see him"—but what's there to see? It's a shame he got his hair cut a day before his death. He was much more handsome with his full white head of hair. Dying people don't need to get their hair cut before their death! It's better for the family if the deceased is remembered with a thick head of hair, rather than with a buzz cut done at home.

Chapter Twelve
The Swearing-In

THEY SAID TO be there at six, because the ceremony starts at seven. It was clear that if the army imposes a time and a place, then that's the reality one must prepare oneself for. Because of the traffic on the coastal road at this time, it was necessary to leave at four-thirty at the latest, perhaps even before. They arrived in two separate cars, the father in one car, and the mother—the Older Daughter—in the other car, in which Iris, her first-born daughter, and Timna, the Younger Daughter of the Only Daughter, would also travel.

Levona, the first-born daughter of the Only Daughter, was on an extended trip in South America, and her grandmother Adele kept track of her route on a large map that she spread out on the dark, sparkling clean wooden table, in the living room of her home on Yehudah Maccabi Street at the corner of Matityahu Cohen Gadol.

Timna, who was already eighteen years old, had arthritis that had gotten worse and worse, and she hadn't grown properly, but remained short instead. Other than this she had osteoporosis in her hip joints, and she also suffered from a weak immune system, and any virus would stick with her for a month.

And on top of all that an eating disorder was added, which was prevalent in the family from the time of the Spanish expulsion, and it hindered her from filling up and rounding out.

Timna was scathing and sharp-witted, like her mother. She knew everything, and it was difficult to withstand such clarity.

Between the Older Daughter and the children's father, who traveled alone in the first car, there was no longer any relationship, and even getting a lift from him to Haifa wasn't possible. The duration of their divorce was nearly equal to the duration of their marriage.

Nadav, their soldier son, would be waiting for them at the naval base dressed in white.

The Older Daughter asked her daughter Iris to ask her father if he was willing to buy the boy a McDonald's hamburger on the way.

No, he will not assist with this thing, answered the father, who began as a sports journalist and over time became the editor of a major weekly magazine. He's traveling straight to the base. Because of the pressure at the magazine he doesn't have time for stops.

That so, they themselves will need to find a McDonald's on the way, but not too early on, so that the hamburger won't arrive cold—the Older Daughter summarized the state of affairs with exaggerated alarm, as is her way, and guided the Hyundai Getz up onto the coastal road.

Her daughter Iris sat next to her, and Timna sat in the back seat. Morale was high, but was occasionally undercut by the fear that the Older Daughter's Isracard Direct credit card wouldn't be approved at the gas station. Then they would have to use Timna's credit card, who was only coming along for the ride, and her father Amatsiah was liable to get angry and see the Older Daughter as an exploiter, bordering on swindler, and thus they would be forced to keep that act absolutely secret.

Pre-paid credit cards have two main problems. Not every place accepts them, and if it does accept them, the computer takes a lot of time to receive approval from the credit card company, and there are long moments of anxiety.

This time, after almost a minute, the Older Daughter heard the cashier approve the purchase of gas, and she was relieved. Although not entirely.

Timna and Iris went to buy diet cola with Timna's credit card. Amatsia wouldn't think the Older Daughter was a "swindler" or a "scoundrel" because of two diet colas. This is what he would call anyone who seemed dubious to him from a social, economic, or moral perspective, and sometimes he would also say "schmuck" or "bitch," depending on the sex of the dubious one.

Now, as the daughters walked away in order to buy the carbonated beverage, Timna's limp was evident. She suffered from excruciating pains in her hip. They say there's no escape from surgery, but they don't know exactly which and where. They're trying other options first.

Less than a day before her death the Only Daughter asked the Older Daughter, in a telephone call to her car, to watch over Levona and Timna after she herself passes to another world. The Older Daughter was just then giving Timna a ride to a private lesson, and Timna too heard the conversation and the mother's crying through the speaker. The Older Daughter was left with no choice but to agree, even though she wasn't qualified to fulfill the request, and the circumstances didn't allow for the keeping of even half the promise.

The Older Daughter tried only here and there. Only here and there.

They didn't happen by a McDonald's anywhere along the coast except for the one inside Rambam Hospital. The Older Daughter couldn't believe that they were again in a hospital parking lot, but Timna, who possesses a superior sense of direction in any and all hospitals, knew how to familiarize herself with Rambam, even though she had never visited it before, and quite quickly came out with Iris and with the hot, packaged hamburger and a regular cola.

Nadav stood with his father near the gate of the base, and at the sight of the three entering through the gate the two began whispering to each other. Their bodies swayed uncomfortably as if saying: get yourselves out of here. Iris gave Nadav the hamburger, but he said he wasn't hungry, he'd hold onto it until later—all the soldiers already ate pizza that the volunteers from the Association for the Well-being of Israel's Soldiers brought.

Other soldiers in white stood with their families. All the families appeared magnificently built, and were equipped with elaborate video cameras. A cold wind blew. Nadav was excited, but insisted on not interacting with his mother in the presence of his father, as if the thing were forbidden.

The Older Daughter was astonished. Wasn't she the mother of this soldier, and why isn't this soldier interacting with her at all?

His father spoke to him and explained the importance of the event, that it's a crossroads in his life as an adult.

There was no possibility of getting close to the boy.

Afterwards all five of them sat around a JNF table, and Nadav forced himself to eat the hamburger. He had a rifle and a cartridge, and the Older Daughter expressed enthusiasm for the weapon and said it's good we have a rifle here, which could be useful, and pointed at the magazine editor and laughed.

"Don't worry, Dad," an amused Nadav reassured him, "If there's a need, I know how to take care of her."

The area for the ceremony was lit by floodlights and stretched out parallel to the sea, the blackened waters of which were at night an outrageous contrast to the naval recruits' white uniforms.

The Older Daughter and the young daughters searched for where to sit according to the placement of Nadav's platoon. From the sea an even colder wind began to blow, and the Older Daughter peeked for the first time at Timna's coat, which became clear to her was nothing but a thin jean jacket. Like her deceased mother, Timna was in the habit of always wearing light clothing, and she was always hot, as was her mother. But now one could see on her face that she was suffering form the cold. The ceremony hadn't yet started, and her face was already white.

The Older Daughter hoped that the ceremony would be

short and that everything would go okay. They watched it in silence. Heard only the whistling wind and the First Sergeant's commands.

Platoons of soldiers dressed in white left the plaza and entered again. An officer invited up an officer subordinate to him, and she marched up right-left and invited up an officer subordinate to her, who invited up an officer subordinate to him, and so on, down to the most subordinate officers, who commanded the recruits' platoons. Timna's lips had turned blue, and the Older Daughter gave her wool jacket to her. Nadav's father photographed him with his smart phone, and sent texts and pictures nonstop to his new wife.

There was an atmosphere of a memorial service and not of a celebratory conclusion to basic training. A few times the crowd was asked to rise and stand on its feet. Once for *yizkor*, and once for the entrance of some officer. And also for the reading of Alterman's poem "The Silver Platter."

And the platoons according to the First Sergeant: attention, at ease, shoulder, flag, eyes front.

Nadav was precise in his movements.

And then someone said two or three words through the loudspeaker and the recruits repeated after him. It's forbidden to put the ceremony up on the internet, but in short: they swore to obey the laws of the country and so on and so forth, and to sacrifice themselves for its sake, and his father takes more and more pictures and sends them to his new wife.

At the end of the ceremony as well, when Nadav ate more pizza and was nice to everyone, the movements of the father were still incomprehensible.

A week of high fever, and after it another five weeks of a deep cough and utter weakness—a month and a half overall—Timna went through. She'll never again in her life go to a sailor's swearing-in ceremony.

Chapter Thirteen
Birmingham Expulsion

It was Sunday morning, and all the soldiers hurried to their bases. With an angry and mainly disappointed face Nadav concluded the latest weekend at home, lifted up his massive duffel bag, got out of the car, slammed its door, and without saying goodbye to his mother who brought him entered the tunnel leading to the train to Haifa.

The Older Daughter made a U-turn and crossed a white line. The taxi drivers at the train's University Station in Tel Aviv stared at her and condoned her with their gaze. Who is the idiotic law-abider who continues all the way to the square and does the whole loop?

The rest of the way home was a traffic jam, and everyone's Hebrew was awful. But that was okay. Let them says what they say however they want.

In addition, half the people were hoarse or had a runny nose, because a cold autumn had begun and all the forecasters said: "Cold for the season."

Both the orthopedist and his honor Rabbi Fierer recommended that Timna have hip replacement surgery in a hospital in Birmingham, which specializes in complex hip transplants. First Timna and her sister Levona traveled with their father for general examinations in Birmingham. Afterward they returned to Israel, and two months later they got a telephone message from Birmingham about a date for the surgery. Now they were about to travel.

The Older Daughter was supposed to go with them to

Birmingham, in order to help Levona roll Timna in a wheelchair in the streets of Birmingham and London, as she had done in Israel, after they returned from the examinations. But at that time the Older Daughter was busy clearing out her house, since she had been forced to sell it because of debts and after she was informed that she had no anticipated revenue for the next fifteen years. Even the honorable tax authorities themselves made her into an exempt dealer instead of a licensed dealer, which she had been until now.

Her daughter Iris moved to an apartment with roommates in Tel Aviv, and she herself and Nadav were about to move into a rented roof apartment. She planned to take wonderful care of the garden, despite the temporariness, and thus, on certain days, there would be pleasure in looking at the flowers and strolling among them and the head-tall sage plants.

In her family they scorned her a lot: everything's temporary with you, and you can't even maintain one hundred and eighty square meters in a residential building near the Green Line.

In the past she would call Adele from time to time to ask her how she was doing, and now too, a few day before the surgery, she called in between packing sessions and told her happily that she's planning on traveling as well, and this way she'll be able to relieve Amatsia and Levona from taking care of Timna. For the ticket she considered using the second payment she was about to receive for the apartment she sold.

But Adele immediately told her that she shouldn't travel to Birmingham in order to help Amatsia and the girls. If she wants a change in scenery, go to Cyprus. There's really great sun there this time of year.

A day after she sent her on vacation to Cyprus, Adele left her a voice message in which she wanted to clarify, that in fact she just means that she doesn't want the Older Daughter to interfere with the connection between the two sisters. An opportunity to nurture and strengthen the relationship between them has fallen into their hands. In a foreign city, after a surgery.

But the connection between the sisters didn't really exist, and how would the Older Daughter interfere with it? On the contrary, she would merely impose peace between them. And at times she fulfilled the Only Daughter's last wishes, to watch over her daughters. It was clear she should travel to Birmingham without any hesitation.

"Go back home," Adele ordered her in her trembling voice. "You're moving apartments, no? So pack up your home and attend to yourself."

Adele nicely put the woman in her place. When the Older Daughter was still a girl Adele identified in her a tendency toward inexhaustible procrastination.

And that wasn't all.

Rina, her neighbor from upstairs, finally received her get, and a few days before the Older Daughter was supposed to leave the Maoz Aviv neighborhood, Rina did some very active pest control. The entire stairwell, including the entrance to the building, as well as the path between the different entrances, filled up with large cockroaches, twitching or already lifeless.

In the middle of the day a white-breasted kingfisher stood on an electric wire with a cockroach in his mouth.

Why doesn't he fly to the Yarkon River, where his place is? Will he call to his friends to come farm the cockroaches? Had their digestive systems become immune in the face of Rina's pesticides?

The dying cockroaches in the stairwell imbued the whole process of packing up the house with a great disquiet, and the Older Daughter took a broom and swept hundreds of them into the garden, for recycling. As the date of the surgery drew closer, she again and again put off the end of the packing and the movers coming, because she thought she'd be launched to Birmingham. But that was only in her head. She remained in Israel with the cardboard boxes and the masking tape. After thirty years in the apartment she had a heavy load, and she didn't plan on sorting through it but rather moving it as it was to the next apartment.

Three days before the surgery, when Amatsia and the girls were already in Birmingham, Adele called the Older Daughter and asked her how she could dare call her a "scoundrel."

"I didn't call you a scoundrel . . . no way."

Adele didn't accept her version, yet agreed to drop the matter. Apparently she remembered vaguely that there was some dispute between them, but not its content.

Two days later, at two Israel-time and twelve England-time, the surgery began. After two and a half hours Adele was already convinced that Timna was no longer with us.

A scream escaped from the Older Daughter's mouth when Adele informed her of this.

"What are you talking about? Of course she's with us."

"She's not with us," Adele insisted over the line.

"She's in surgery for a hip replacement! It takes time. Amatsia said that if the surgery lasts a while, it's a sign that they're replacing the entire joint!"

"But why isn't it like in Israel," she said in a trembling voice, "the doctors come out every fifteen minutes and say what's happening. No-no. The girl isn't alive."

"Of course she's alive. Stop talking like that."

"How great for you that you can think like that. How great . . ."

After four hours the surgery ended successfully. In regards to *this* hip—quiet had been achieved for the next fifteen years.

Twelve days later the father and his daughters returned to Israel. Timna was hospitalized at Tel-Hashomer for rehabilitation, and Amatsia gradually switched to a twice-a-week round trip, Ramat-Aviv-Tel-Hashomer, instead of every day.

A month passed, two months passed, and suddenly it became clear to the Older Daughter that an old-new character was playing the lead role without her knowledge, whereas she herself was only in the position of a passing clown possessing underlying charlatanry, and not a word from her mouth should be believed.

Drora McKay is a cousin of the Only Daughter, rest in peace, on Adele's side, but she hadn't been heard from intensively even at the worst of times, since she lived in Edinburgh with her husband, the Scottish Lord McKay.

But they knew about Drora McKay. For instance, they knew there was no one like Drora McKay. They knew that Drora McKay had nailed her part at her surprise wedding to a Lord back in the early eighties, and that she in fact became a Lady. Lord McKay was a man perched up high and with a different look. And in general, he was a man who was careful about what he wore—if only it were that way for all of us; he would come to funerals in a record-breaking heat wave with a blazer, tie, and some black hat.

Due to her considerations, decades old, Adele didn't want the Older Daughter and Drora McKay to rub against each other, and indeed for years they barely saw one another—at funerals Drora came to with the Lord or sometimes alone.

The McKay family didn't live in Birmingham, but they had some footing there, in contrast to the Older Daughter, who didn't have half of nothing with that place.

And McKay indeed proved herself and arranged an apartment for Amatsia and the girls in Birmingham, for the period of the surgery and recovery. And look now another cat is suddenly out of the bag: Amazia revealed to the Older Daughter that Adele said openly that she doesn't want the Older Daughter to reside in the apartment that Drora McKay arranged. Therefore Adele then gave her a "dose" as she put it: that she stay in her place and do with her home like anyone else, that is: continue packing your apartment—and she retreated, ashamed and beaten, from her plans to travel to Birmingham.

The night of *seder* arrived. The familial rending was as follows: Amatsia and his daughters traveled to friends on a kibbutz. Iris and Nadav traveled to the Younger Daughter, who conducts a proper life style and has known all her life how to navigate true dramas and volatility nicely. Recently she became a devout believer in the evil eye, and therefore she hides all sorts of things she's bought or done, other than renovations that are impossible to hide.

And of course, Vivienne also spent the night of the *seder* with the Younger Daughter.

Whereas the Older Daughter went to two friends in central Tel Aviv.

Nadav and Iris drove her there in her car, because it was impossible to get a cab—at all the big taxi stands the phone rang without anyone picking up, as if wishing to say "there are no cabs." Afterward Nadav and Iris continued in her own car to the Younger Daughter, and picked up Vivienne on their way. There was a silent agreement that it was better for the Older Daughter not to come to the Younger Daughter's, because she was liable to ruin everything. The Older Daughter didn't want to ruin anything, but she ruined and how. She got off at the intersection, and looked at the car receding with her children, whom her mother would join in a bit, and all of them would head north until Kfar Saba.

Upstairs, on the sixth floor, the friends took pains to make a healthy meal, but the Older Daughter suddenly felt very bad. Something deep, unresolved, between her and herself. And besides this, there was a *red* tablecloth on the table, and in the *menorah* on the windowsill eight Hanukah candles and the *shammas* were lit, and on the table there wasn't a single piece of matza. Everything was eclectic as far as the holidays were concerned.

But neither the menorah nor the absence of matza caused her to weep. After two glasses of wine she unpacked an inner load of bitter tears in front of the two who labored so hard over the meal. They calmed her down and returned to some of the *seder* to the best of their ability. One brought a cup of water. The other said, "I don't understand." Eventually the better friend from among the two of them brought her to an already-empty cab that passed below, and with a worried face, but glad for the liberation awaiting him, said to the driver: "Take the woman to 124 . . ." and slammed the door with spiritual relief.

But the great outsider on the night of that *seder* was old Adele, who remained in bed alone with her Filipina's nursing, and gazed at the ceiling. For a few months already she's refused to get up out of her bed, and fixes her gaze on the ceiling. No longer interacts with the world, can't bear a world without Vita and the Only Daughter. She refuses to watch television as well, and she's merely cold all the time. Or she's hot, and she has a small, colorful fan that circulates the air for her. And alternatively, a convector that pumps out warm air.

A struggle broke out in the family that didn't reach the courts. In the end Amatsia won a share of Adele's inheritance, that is, he officially got his apartment, which was registered to his deceased wife's parents even when the Only Daughter was still alive. And now here, as the exclusive owners of the property, and theoretically also the owners of another two apartments that will be inherited in due course—his outlook changed radically and he doesn't allow Levona and Timna to even speak with her, lest it upset the new social order.

She tries to communicate with them over the phone and through Facebook, but they block her. Fine, maybe he does allow them, and it only seems that way to her, but they no longer are interested in her company.

A full year passed since the first Birmingham expulsion. Now they're preparing to replace Timna's hip on the other side. But there's no point in calling Amazia or Timna and Levona. Those two have dismissed the Older Daughter, with or without his encouragement.

She didn't ask to join the second round in Birmingham at all. She was informed of the details by Adele, who again fell flat on her face while her Filipina caretaker was out jogging in

Hayarkon Park. Who knows how long she waited for her on the floor.

During the Older Daughter's visit she lay without moving, recovering, in a bed with floral sheets—dark blue flowers on a white background. On her right and her left were gray chests with many drawers connected to a rectangular headboard—all of it Formica. In the deceased Only Daughter's bed the Filipina would sleep. The daughter's bed remained as it had been in her youth.

"Let it be over already, let it be over!" she said to the Older Daughter.

And this one first mumbled something like, "hold on," but said in her heart: "Surely she doesn't want to hold on," and therefore said to her in the end:

"May it all pass easily."

When she stood up to leave Olivia the Filipina caregiver called for the elevator with the turn of a key. A key like this was in the hands of only a portion of the residents in the building on Yehudah Hamaccabi, as only this portion of the building's residents funded the installation of the elevator, and the others were not allowed to use it.

Many days like this and others passed, and a very hot day arrived in which all the air was scalding and people dragged themselves feebly up the day's incline. After a not so short rift between her and that side of the family the Older Daughter finally arrived to visit Adele. She pressed on the name Kastil on the intercom, and there was no answer. She stubbornly pressed again, after all it wasn't possible that the Filipina went out jogging on a very hot day like this as well. Suddenly she heard Adele's voice on the intercom asking, "Who is it?" and she answered, but on the other end of the line silence prevailed.

She was almost certain that Adele fell after answering the intercom. Therefore the Older Daughter called Olivia's cell phone, and voicemail answered. She called Adele's apartment, the landline, and after many rings reached voicemail here as well. It was clear to her that Adele fell and is lying helpless on the spotlessly clean terrazzo floor. All that remained was getting an answer to the question where did she get hurt and what's her condition.

She called Amatsia. A few months before this they had a big fight, and since then he'd been boycotting her.

But he actually answered the telephone, and immediately called Olivia's new number, who it turned out was shopping at the supermarket.

For about five minutes the Older Daughter waited, sitting frozen on the tiled steps of the building's entryway, wrapped up in the knowledge that she was the one who caused the fall. And then, as if in miraculous fashion, Olivia urgently appeared, with two large, full plastic bags from the supermarket on each wrist, and hurried to type in the building's entry code.

"I am sure she fell," the Older Daughter told her in broken English, "I needed to inform in the phone before I'm coming."

They hurried upstairs. Olivia opened the door and immediately ran to the left, but when she saw that Adele's bed was empty, she turned in horror to the right, put the bags on the floor, and called to Adele by name.

Adele lay conscious on the living room floor, and the Older Daughter asked her essential questions, like where does it hurt you. Olivia put a pillow under her head and neck, and she moaned.

"You shouldn't touch her," the Older Daughter said to Olivia, who wanted to lift her up.

"I'm ordering an ambulance for you," the Older Daughter said when finally the light went on in her head, and Adele nodded her head as much as the position and pain would allow.

At the ER in Ichilov Hospital Adele said that she hadn't seen a living soul (other than Olivia) for two weeks already, and thus all that was left to her was speaking to abstract entities, who would come to help her. Recently she spoke with her mother, who died in the sixties.

Fortunately she had no fractures. Not in her back or limbs.

A few days later she was released, and another period of disconnection between her and the Older Daughter prevailed. But one day the Older Daughter decided that despite the anxiety that these visits induce in her, she's taken her distance from Adele too far. For too long she hadn't set foot in Yehudah Hamaccabi corner of Matitiyah-Cohen-Gadol fourth floor. This time she informed the Filipina that she was coming. Adele lay in bed. The bedding had dainty, light-blue flowers, and again the background was white.

From time to time Adele still struggled with the pains from that fall, and she faced the ceiling, because all other positions caused her hellish pains. Behind her were hanging pictures of all the family members in a jumble—the dead and the living, the healthy and the sick.

She said, "Do you know that Timna grew seven centimeters since the surgeries in Birmingham?"

"Wonderful," the uninvited but desired guest was happy, and continued to sit there, and told Adele all sorts of stories from the past, and Adele smiled brightly at the ceiling, because the Older Daughter reminded her of her glory days, how she would travel to the Weizmann Institute each day to her chemist's job, and how she drove the daughters of the sick, Only Daughter to wherever they wanted—clubs, the country club pool on Bavli, private lessons.

After an hour she got up to leave, and sadness could be seen on Olivia's face as well.

"You'll come again?" Adele asked.

"Yes."

"Promise?"

"Yes."

"Even a half-hour is enough."

But the Older Daughter barely came, and the granddaughters also barely came. One's studying for a master's, the other is studying for the entrance exams, while the Older Daughter—she will forever have a negative balance with Adele and the girls.

Chapter 14
The Spring of Riots

When Fareed Al-Amrawi was ten years old he stood at his full height, which was a bit short relative to children his age, facing the Pyramids in Giza, and saw them as he always saw them (he originally saw them from the height of his father's shoulders). As in the past he wondered at this wonder of the world, but a thought about the inside of the Pyramids suddenly shot through his mind. Not about the casing, nor about the tombs buried inside, and not about the inner sanctums, but rather about those hidden stones that can't be seen at all.

Isn't it the case that ancient workers also sailed the heavy granite stones that fill the Pyramids' unseen interior on barges from distant quarries in the southern Nile, just like the granite stones of the casing, only the latter received an exterior finish, because those you see, whereas the ones filling the interior, the ones buried deep at the back for thousands of years, and the ones that do most of the hard work of bearing the burden of the entire pyramid—those are usually forgotten. Those rocks are discriminated against compared to their friends, and this injustice is eternal—Al-Amrawi thought—just like the Pyramids themselves. His heart ached for the fate of the anonymous, exiled rocks, which most tourists generally don't bother to think about either.

At his parents' home in Cairo the boy arrived to the conclusion that there's nothing to be done—the rules of geometric space sentence the interior of the Khufu, Khafre, and Menkaure pyramids to silence and darkness. Al-Amrawi's mind was advanced relative to his contemporaries. Both the children and the teachers excluded him from the accepted bunch and left him with an emotional wound because of this as well. Indeed his height shot up suddenly in adolescence and he wound up in the average range, but by then it was already too late.

After a being ostracized a few times at school, and in order to keep himself from getting mixed up in altercations with name-calling kids stronger than him, he found a trick for calming himself down completely and for a long time. He would concentrate and develop thoughts about the interior of the pyramids, about the giant, mysterious granite stones, which live in hiding and hold up the pyramids without moving—and he identified with their greatness. From this he also concluded that perseverance, stubbornness, and diligence would be at their best when concealed from view. He adopted this conclusion as a mantra, and inserted it into his existence, his appearance, his walk, and his stance. He didn't leave home from so much laboring over books on ancient Egyptian history, and barely ate either, and over the years looked more and more like a nimble web spinner. From the outside it appeared that he was apathetic and in possession of infinite calm, but inside his soul quaked and teemed like an anthill and waited to burst forth like a monster in a well-made movie.

He developed into a solitary and very ambitious person. Already by age thirteen he succeeded in climbing to the top of the great Khufu pyramid, and he wrote the date and time at the top for himself. Four previous tries were unsuccessful, and this was the fifth try.

It was a spring day, a light wind blew, but when he reached the top of the pyramid the wind mussed up his black curls, and he moved a curl from his eyes in order to better see what could be viewed from above.

He was happy. The air of the peaks filled his lungs again and again, until he felt a bit dizzy. Most of Cairo was spread out at his feet—Cairo Tower, the Saladin Citadel, and the Television Building. And to the south—Saqqara. He stayed up there for a few long minutes, and then quickly descended.

He never again scaled the tops of the pyramids. Not Khufu and not Khafre and not Menkaure, but he read many books about them. As someone who did not get along with people living in the present, he read fervently about the past peoples of Egypt and the glory of their culture. The fact that Egypt is the cradle of civilization instilled him with pride, because he sensed a genetic proximity to this cradle.

He was quite sorry he didn't live in the time of the Pharaohs. It seemed to him that he was well suited to live the life of a pharaonic king, or at least the life of one of the honorable members of his court. And he excelled so much in his studies at primary school, even in the real subjects, to the point that afterward, in high school, they gave him approval to study the regular classes simultaneously with courses in archeology and history at Cairo University.

Naturally afterward he went to study Egyptology and finished his BA. And then the peace agreement between Israel and Egypt was signed and he answered an announcement on behalf of the Israeli embassy for a fellowship at Tel Aviv University.

The answer did not take long to come: accommodations plus a living stipend for two semesters.

In the Tel Aviv of the early eighties El-Amwari felt free as he never had felt before in his life. When he returned to his homeland he already spoke Hebrew well, and immediately began working as a tour guide for Israeli tourists, who in those days visited Egypt en masse. He would speak elevated, cautious and a bit hesitant, but exemplary Hebrew, and would weave in new words as well, which he learned form the Israeli newspapers he read, and slang expressions that he absorbed form the tourists themselves. And he had not only economic security, but even saved for a rainy day.

Frequently he escorted and gave a tour to some important Israeli, or two important ones, with their entourage, whose visit in Egypt was more discreet.

He had a set route, the beginning of which was the Giza

pyramids, and continued onto the Saqqara pyramids, and back to Cairo—Khan el-Khalili market (where Israelis bought mainly scarves), afterwards he would take the tourists to the Egyptian Museum, and finally—the highpoint of the visit in the eyes of many of the Israelis—the Coptic churches, and the ancient Ben-Ezra synagogue in the Jewish Quarter (Harat al-Yahud), in whose attic the *genizah* was found, something that proved to Israelis that even Cairo's ancient quarter belonged to them.

Only El-Amwari's familiarity with the biblical books of Ezra and Nehemia, and his expertise in important controversies in Judaism over the centuries, prevented fairly well any possible agitation against him among the Israeli groups, who didn't know a thing about these things, or in the best case had only highly superficial knowledge, and here was an Egyptian, with exactly the same cheekbones that Anwar Sadat had, standing before them and speaking with them in Hebrew, and mixing his speech with words and expressions in Aramaic that they themselves didn't understand, and who knew about the fights between the *Chasidim* and the *Mitnagdim*.

In those fine days El-Amwari was exposed to all sorts of Israelis, and found an anthropologic interest in their surging mastery over every place the stepped into. Their ancestors built the pyramids when they were slaves in Egypt. The Nile was somehow theirs as well, because Moses floated in an ark on it. More than once there were the nervy among them who asked him if the contemporary Egyptian is the same as the ancient Egyptian, or if the contemporary Egyptian is a descendent of a wild tribe that arrived on camels from the desert, after the ancient Egyptians had been annihilated.

"Contemporary Egyptians are the direct offspring of the ancient Egyptians," he repeated, and once in fact compared his face to the face of a mummy in the Egyptian Museum.

But overall he liked the Israelis and found a common language with them, even though he had never seen arrogance like theirs, to which was added a very forgiving attitude toward him, something that caused in him, albeit only on rare occasions, a feeling of alienation and disgust. He learned to discern who among them was from Haifa and who from Jerusalem or a kibbutz, and even who was a Tel Avivian from birth and who had just hitched a ride into that city.

Fareed's complaints from those days now seem to him to have belonged to another person. In those days he also managed to buy himself a small apartment in Cairo. In the beginning even the pyramids could be seen through his windows, or part of them, until a wave of construction hid everything. And when over the years Israeli tourists dwindled, he found for himself, Fareed did, other tourists, and from among all of them he preferred the Jewish tourists.

So his life progressed for over a quarter-century, and perhaps it would have continued flowing onward like this, were it not for the Egyptian Spring. A burst of adrenaline the likes of which he had never known before flooded him during the days of the independence protests in Tahrir Square. El-Amwari lost control of himself and waved his arms together with the masses. But in November 2011 a dramatic change occurred in his attitude toward these protests. On that day the Egyptian army opened with live fire on the protesters. A bullet whistled by El-Amwari's ear and penetrated the neck of the man running in front of him. His blood sprayed onto El-Amwari, who wanted to offer him help but wasn't able—the shots were close and frequent, and he continued to run, until he reached his home through side streets.

All this very much shook up the tour guide. A few changes in his personality may have even taken place. He became quieter. And unemployed.

This was a period of survival. There were no more open Israelis in Egypt, not in the embassy nor in institutes of any kind, and even curious tourists of other nationalities barely came, not even from Arab countries, which had been shaken as well in the new winds of the Spring.

Due to these changes in his life he weakened physically, and would stretch out on the couch most days. He drained all his savings, and had already started thinking about schemes for making money.

El-Amwari understood that he was buried deep inside the Arab Spring, and who knew how long this spring would last. His livelihood had gone to hell, and he was out of ideas for how to acquire another twenty lira. And even the friends from whom he had borrowed money demanded their money back.

Since that shooting incident he thoroughly considered whether to go out into the streets again with everyone or stay by himself at home on the couch and watch the happenings in the street via television and the Internet.

Sometimes he would hear what was happening in the streets near his apartment, and a moment later would hear the things again on his television, or read about them on Facebook.

He would often think about the man whose neck the bullet pierced. He had no chance to save him, and if he had hung around in order to stop the man's blood, he would have quite quickly caught a bullet, and then there would be two dead. The decision was immediate, in a tenth of a second and without thinking—and he remained alive, and now did not know how to fund the remainder of his existence.

The few times he turned for help to the Israeli embassy, which knew well to use him during the glory days, he got an answering machine that instructed him to call after the holidays, but there was no Jewish holiday on the horizon.

He went back to smoking after quitting for ten years. His hair grew wild, and he slept frequently. When he would awake he felt a loss of identity, fear, and finally disillusionment and despair. He lost a lot of weight in those days, and looked like someone stricken by a severe illness.

The Cairo Zoo was established in the nineteenth century, and the condition of the animals in it, in the days of the riots, was as if they too were out of the nineteenth century: almost lifeless skin and bones, in rusty cages, of the sort animals haven't been housed in for some time because of their tininess. The turtle's pool was the size of his shell. Dryness, disappointment, and stench prevailed over everything, the surrounding vegetation withered, and only the trees that gave shade still stood there. The grass, which in normal times was green, upon which families would hold picnics for hours, turned yellow and was nearly empty of people. In days like these, when there's shooting in the streets, people don't risk it to come to the zoo with their kids.

This is totally normal, Fareed El-Amwari said to himself when he entered the zoo gates following an ad he saw on the Internet, which said that they were looking for a manager and no previous experience was necessary. He called and they told him to come. At first he thought about not going, but in the end he went. Went and got the job on the spot. After a brief tour of the zoo alone it was hard for him to believe that things had gotten to this point. As in all of Egypt, chaos prevailed also in the zoo.

This mythological zoo had already lost its greatness many years earlier. The cages hadn't been enlarged, and the animals grew skinnier and skinnier. Abdallah the young veterinarian, who not so recently completed his studies in Rome, Italy, joined the zoo staff right before the spring of riots, and had a severe nervous breakdown due to a series of tragic events.

First things first, the new manager El-Amwari ordered a general cleaning operation and a separation of the corpses from the living. Second, he enforced the zoo's central rule—ever since he was a boy he remembered the signs: feeding the animals is forbidden. In the past special guards patrolled the grounds, whose job it was to enforce order and see to it that the animals ate only the food that the zoo itself assigned to them, and in exchange for a modest *baksheesh* let the children throw a few peanuts or a banana to the monkeys. But there were no more guards like this now, and ever since the weakening of the old order all sorts of animal lovers and weirdos came to the zoo, who fed the animals everything imaginable.

The monkeys suffered from diarrhea, and it was as if the hyenas had rusted out and matched themselves to their cages. El-Amwari had a pocket notebook back from the times he was a tour guide at the pyramids and the floating Coptic Church, and he went from cage to cage and took notes. He found that the tiger had lost all the contrast in his fur, grown very skinny, and in general didn't look like a tiger, but rather a large cat with bones not belonging to him. And the caracal, even if you waved a dead rabbit in front of its eyes, wouldn't budge from his spot. In a rectangular cage, long and narrow, he saw two lions and four lionesses pacing here and there in the narrow space. Two of the four lionesses had cataracts, this was so clear, and the lion, oh, the lion—hundreds of flies gathered around him, because of a rotting wound on his leg that was spreading, and driving him mad. He opened his mouth to roar, but only the end of a growl was to be heard. The gray crocodile clung to the cage's glass and ignored all the other attractions around it: three stones and two castor oil shrubs that grew among them. The manager stood across from it for some time and didn't know if it was living or the work of a taxidermist—because it didn't move at all. Finally, after he banged forcefully on the window, it agreed to move its upper body a bit. The pool of the sea turtle was so green that you couldn't make out the turtle unless it moved one of its limbs. A thin snake was hanging from a branch exactly in the middle of its abdomen, half of it here and half of it there, and its condition couldn't be known without a thorough examination. The flamingos, whose pink intensifies when in captivity, had turned almost red in this zoo, and standing before them the one-time tour guide noted that an urgent blood examination should be conducted for the flamingos and the rest of the animals. Street cats wandered among the flamingos and searched for which among them had grown weak today, but fortunately for the flamingos the street cats also suffered from exhaustion.

But in the days to come the situation grew worse yet. The

ostriches were traumatized by the sound of shootings in the city streets, sometimes in the street right next to the zoo. After an especially turbulent night more than half of them died from an illness that had symptoms of flu, but was apparently caused by panic. That same night the elephant was wounded by a bullet, albeit superficially, but there was a need to care for it as well. The monkeys had terrible shrieking spasms. The rhinoceros looked as if it were having awful stomachaches. In short, Fareed arrived at the conclusion that there was no escape but to nevertheless try and summon Abdallah, the broken-down veterinarian, to the scene. Abdallah actually cooperated and was happy to leave home after such a long time. Returning to work was good for him, and he went back to caring for the animals devotedly, as he thought was necessary. But even though he arrived at work almost every day, and appeared to be back on track, and even succeeded in healing the rhinoceros—he disappeared after a month, and didn't return calls. The full burden of the fate of the zoo's animals now fell on El-Amwari, the one-time tour guide, mainly for Israelis, and he tried his best to improve their condition.

One day, a bit after the elections that replaced the old ruler with a new ruler who would himself also be replaced soon, El-Amwari stood in the zoo, planted on his spot, marveling at and lacking explanations for the order of the world. A great excitement seized him. Was the svelte woman, who was standing next to the fallow deer and feeding them something that from a distance looked like stuffed grape leaves, actually Celeste Sanuah, daughter of the legendary head of the Jewish community, Annette Sanuah, who passed away at the age of ninety-one a bit after the old regime fell? For years the older Sanuah had made a stink about introducing a women's section to the Ben-Ezra Synagogue. She was a dominant woman—*choleshet* in Hebrew—even though that root in Hebrew meant weakness, and her daughter was now dominant, thought the one-time tour guide.

He once saw a photo of the two of them in the *Al-Ahram* newspaper, in a column on the city's wealthy and notable residents. In the same column it was also noted that the mother and daughter own many homes throughout the city. From the period in which he escorted Israeli tourists through the city he knew the mother had the key for that same women's section, and through a hole in its wall people once crawled through the dust to the attic where the *genizah* was found, the one worth millions upon millions.

When he visited the Ben-Ezra Synagogue with the Israeli tourists he saw that most of them hadn't heard about the *genizah* and didn't know about their own history. More than once El-Amwari wanted to tell them that they're ignorant and uneducated people, but he didn't dare. He was astounded to see that their general lack of knowledge didn't prevent the Israelis from sensing ownership of the Ben-Ezra Synagogue as well, since the Rambam would pray in it.

El-Amwari's thinking was very fast. Sometimes he knew what a person was about to say after saying only two words. Now too his mind worked insanely fast and connected one thing to another.

Here is an exceptionally tall, thin woman, except for the wide hips. Her rear end is relatively large but disappointingly flat and not vivacious.

Everything really was a matter of genes. Celeste inherited the length of her body from her father, who died while she was still a child. He was six feet, three-inches tall and represented Egypt in sprinting at the Olympics. He passed on his knack for running to her as well, but she didn't dare go out jogging in the streets of Cairo, and she would run on the home treadmill, her hair gathered in a ponytail bouncing this way and that. She inherited her relatively wide hips from her mother. She was good-looking, but wasn't strikingly beautiful like her mother. Her face was too big to accentuate the perfect facial features the deceased had, the features were lost in hers.

She always felt discomfort from physically towering over

everyone. Ach. If they would only take half a foot from her!

Her feet were also large, and her shoes were size 43, European.

She was an only child, because immediately after she was born the mother Annette decided not to bring any more children into the world. God forbid her other daughters, she didn't want there to be competition between sisters in her home (she herself had two sisters, who moved to Marseilles and married wealthy men). But despite being an only child Celeste wasn't spoiled. Annette ruled the house with ironclad discipline, which she called "European." Celeste's father did indeed die from a heart attack many years earlier, but when she was a girl he taught to her to have mercy on animals, and would breach his wife's rules of discipline and allow his daughter to feed the animals at the zoo.

And she continued to feed the animals after his death to this day. Fareed didn't dare look close up at what she was pulling out for them from the bag she held in her hand—due to confusion.

And in fact before he finally identified her El-Amwari wanted to shout at her, "Ma'am, feeding the animals is forbidden," but the woman turned her wide, pleasant face to him, and opposite her large, white smile, and opposite the flowery scarf that she wore on her head and tied under her chin in an effort to bestow upon her face an outline that would reduce the all-in-all of it—he first opened up and said with dignity and grace:

"Greetings to you, Miss Sanuah. I, Fareed El-Amwari, sympathize with you over the death of your mother Annette."

Celeste maintained a serious expression, but there was joy in her heart. Finally they're calling her Miss Sanuah! She instantly grew happy, and was already emotionally open for what might come next.

"Thank you," Celeste said and her face lit up. Her walking and standing were a bit bent over, and it appeared hard for her to drag around that large internal area of hers. She wiped from her hands the remains of the food she gave to the fallow deer on a napkin she herself embroidered.

Reading and embroidery would calm Celeste, who always felt

that she and being don't necessarily go hand in hand. She had a lovely garden, where she read and embroidered as well. It had a sixty-plus year-old Egyptian palm tree with six large branches. Her father planted it a few days after she was born.

"Thanks for the condolences," she said with slightly forced graciousness, "and forgive me for not remembering you," she apologized for no reason, "many people visited after my mother's death."

She was a head and a half taller than him, and it wasn't possible to cut off that head. All her life that head had separated her from everyone else. This head, in her opinion, was also what prevented her from marrying and bringing children into the world. Men don't like women taller than them, her mother always told her, and she was right. Very slowly, starting from about age ten, Celeste began a long process of self-denial, and everything that her severe mother predicted—came to be.

In her twenties and thirties, thanks to her mother's matchmaking efforts, she had a few terrible experiences with men, who lead her to passivity, to the point that she didn't work out of the house and at home had maids who would do everything. She passed her days with her reading and embroidery, with sewing if needed, and by sleeping much more than she needed to. There were periods she embroidered and periods she did not, but her mind was always working, because she was always reading some book. What hadn't she read during all those years? She was familiar with the great works of Italian, French, Russian, and American literature. She read them, and read them again. They had a massive library. What was translated into Arabic she read in Arabic, and what wasn't translated, she read in the Italian that she knew from childhood. And each and every book in their beautiful library, with glass doors, she insisted on wrapping in clear plastic, in order to preserve them.

Celeste learned the craft of fine embroidery directly from her mother, and so, many times, the two would sit across from the television, each one with her embroidery in her hand. Lately she embroiders patterns of flowers that she downloads from the Internet onto black satin, and afterwards sews lovely pillows out of them, which are closed up imperceptibly with pleated snaps. It goes without saying that she's a virtuoso not only with handmade things, but also with machine embroidery and sewing. Now she orders threads and needles from France on the Internet, and within two days they arrive.

For a few years Celeste lived outside the large house, in various apartments they owned in Cairo, but in the end, when her mother reached eighty, she returned to the large house, in order to be with her mother in her final years—so she explained to herself.

Neither the mother Annette nor the daughter Celeste had any tie to the state of Israel. Just the opposite, they strictly avoided contact with their brethren from across the desert, or with their emissaries in Cairo. They immediately threw the invitations for Israeli holidays from the embassy into the garbage. In their own eyes they were Jewish-Egyptian, belonging to the Egyptian people.

"Feeding the animals is forbidden here," the manager finally said.

"You work here?" Celeste asked and didn't wait for his response. "Yes, feeding the animals is forbidden," she pointed at a worn-out sign on which that was written, "but how can one not? Have pity on them, see what they look like."

"The zoo workers feed them," the manager said automatically and continued following after her, and kept quiet in the presence of the hyenas falling upon the scraps of meat she now threw to them. Celeste fed the hyenas cut-up chicken necks, and El-Amwari got a headache. They fell upon the food the second time she threw it at them as well.

"They're dying of hunger," Celeste said.

"Apparently they forgot about them today," Fareed tried to explain.

He immediately identified in her a heartrending weakness and a great need for love and recognition and decided not to argue with her.

And only now did he introduce himself as a tour guide, who at the moment is working as the zoo manager, since these days there aren't any tourists, but someone has to take care of the animals.

She looked at least ten years older than him. Maybe more. It was reasonable to assume that she's over sixty, but still in shape, and how her height diminished him. He wondered if she were married, but immediately understood that if she were married, her husband wouldn't allow her to wander around a zoo alone these days, even if she very much felt sorry for the animals.

"I'll check into the matter of animal feedings today," he said and planned to call in with his old Nokia device and to use an authoritative voice and deliver instructions, but he saw that the battery was dead, and so he said goodbye to her and returned to his office.

The evening of that same day, unlike his habit of staying closed-up at home, he went out to the streets to see what was happening and where. The streets, even the main ones, were quiet, and he walked rather calmly. He had a good, buoyant feeling, that there's hope. While walking he found that he could fall in love with her easily. He would get trapped in her net, and even if it were a slightly worn-out net—what of it? He too was tired of life. He actually found it very helpful, because she could no longer bring children into the world. That is, she wouldn't trap him.

Her eyes that he saw today were large and beautiful and radiated a cold pleasantness. You could see on her that her heart had been broken a few times in her life, El-Amwari thought, and her coldness didn't deter him. The world has changed, he said to himself, and you must expect much less from people.

About once a week Celeste arrived to feed the animals, sometimes even with disposable gloves, which she insisted on getting rid of while still at the zoo. Once she got carried away and brought kebab for the lions. They ate it immediately, and the lion tried to roar, but in the end a yawn came out of its mouth. She brought rice for the deer, and nuts for the monkeys. Until one day she appeared only with the necks from the butcher for the predators, and Corn Flakes for the others, and Fareed wondered about the meaning of the change, and if it indicated some change in her financial condition, or perhaps it was a passing caprice, following something she read on the Internet.

And then another bloody day arrived, in which her accountant was killed. He was wounded by a bullet during a demonstration challenging the legality of the previous elections. Celeste was shocked. She hadn't yet managed to finish digesting the death of Annette, her dear mother, and here Dionysus, the half-Greek, trusted ally of the family, is killed as well. She stopped going out of the house, not even to the zoo. The loss of the mother and the loss of the loyal accountant in the same year were in her eyes reality's macabre concoction for someone whose life wasn't great to begin with.

She fired the cook and the gardener, because she didn't want them to see her on a daily basis. Their presence distressed her at certain times, because they forced manners onto her when she herself only wanted to crawl back into bed. But she kept the Coptic cleaning woman, twice a week, half of the house each time. And she started developing new fears, and was especially afraid of opening envelopes that arrived in the mail. Actually she developed a fear of dealing with bureaucracy, and this piled up on itself. Her mother had always dealt with bills and finances, and she passed it on immediately to Dionysus. For many years Annette praised him to her daughter, and Celeste knew as well now: Dionysus, Dionysus, Dionysus.

But Dionysus was gone, and in the accountant's office was welter and waste. Good friends, friends that could perhaps be mobilized to help on days like these, she, Celeste, didn't have either, other than a few bores from the Jewish community, who saw her as a bridge to Annette and not as someone in her own right, and who disappeared with the death of her mother.

One day—a day that began as a not warm day—Celeste appeared again by surprise at the zoo with a few necks in a plastic box, and told Fareed, with tears in her eyes, about the death of the accountant. And immediately she removed sunglasses from her bag, and Fareed wondered if her expensive sunglasses were also prescription, and if she personally brought them from Switzerland.

On this visit they strolled from cage to cage, and he presented to her improvements that he had introduced, and she told him that she finally removed her deceased mother's items from the house, and he said to himself that it's reasonable to assume that she has a psychologist, because that's the instruction of a psychologist.

Celeste didn't remember the last time she had real interest in a man, and her talents in the area were not exceptional. The relationships she had in practice were bumbling and not always permissible. For example, for years in her mind and soul she was closely attached to some professor, a lecturer in Philosophy at Cairo University, married, whom she met during the period of her studies there, whereas he didn't pay attention to her at all, despite her youth and beauty. He would appear to her in her dreams, and she had to be satisfied with that—until with the passage of time she lost interest in him. Indeed, most of the men the soul of the Egyptian Jew desired were impossible, and most of them were across the sea, such as the one she met in Corsica on vacation with Annette, and pursued in her imagination for two years, until she let him escape from her head and return to his life.

If she had acquiesced to her mother, she would have been married with children for some time, but she herself forcefully took her virginity dispassionately at the age of eighteen, after her mother suggested for her a Jewish businessman, thirty-two years old, from a good family in Morocco, who wanted a Jewish virgin.

And here, next to the Egyptian with the ancient facial features, who works at the zoo, she miraculously felt an ease she hadn't felt with a man, perhaps because of his true profession—tour guide. Celeste looked at him and wanted to be a tourist with him. She thought that she was already finished, but he kindles the life in her. Suddenly she wants a friend for certain hours of the day, a sort of shadow whose existence isn't stressed too much, in contrast to her mother's dominance. In truth, a Jewish woman in Cairo needs someone to protect her. But what does she want from him exactly? Why is this Egyptian burning up her cheeks? She's blushing.

"It got hot all of a sudden," El-Amwari said. "It was pleasant before, and I had already figured a nice day arrived, with a little breeze."

"I agree with you," Celeste said, "it warmed up suddenly. Mercy on these animals, really."

Beads of sweat pooled on his forehead. She glanced at his face and again identified the ancient Egyptian in it, whom she learned about in school and saw more than once in her visits as a high school student to the Egyptian Museum.

"That being the case, how are you managing?" El-Amwari asked and looked up at her face.

"God is great," Celeste said.

But he demanded to know who handles her affairs, and she told him that at the accountants' office they moved her into the hands of a young worker, a novice.

El-Amwari wrinkled his forehead and said:

"It's not good that your affairs are in the hands of a novice. How do you know that he's good at all?"

He hoped that Celeste's loneliness would drop her into his hands. His loneliness had by now already exhausted him quite a bit.

More time passed than you might think before it happened, and the distress of loneliness didn't work to his advantage, but another distress did. Celeste began receiving confiscation notices from the torn state. There were battles in the streets—but the debt collectors were like clockwork. She neglected the incoming mail, and the thing came back at her like a boomerang.

"You don't know what's going on with me," she told Fareed opposite the fallow deer's cage. "Papers on the bureau at the entrance, piles of bills, envelopes closed up and sealed in the drawers. After mother's death, when Dionysus was still alive, I would pass all the mail on to him without opening it. But I can't pass all my mail on to a novice accountant, who I don't exactly know. I wasn't prepared for Dionysus's death."

"That really wasn't okay on his part," El-Amwari smiled, and again a fire was lit in Celeste's cheeks.

The fallow deer gather before her, but she forgot to feed them.

By the giraffes Celeste soon told him about the seizures due to the payments that she had no idea needed to be made. She's drowning in bureaucratic papers, and she needs the help of someone organized, who was ready to run for her.

It's clear that Celeste wasn't a dummy. She checked him out first. She let him organize the debts to the city of Cairo, and he took care of the matter in a flash and was found to be efficient and curious. She opened the drawers before him and showed him the amount of mail she received and hadn't opened since the death of her mother, and he was stunned at first, but magnanimously agreed to take the mail to his home and look at it over three days and tell her what was important and what wasn't.

In short, at the age of sixty-five, three months after her accountant was killed at a demonstration, Celeste appointed El-Amwari as a sort of junior accountant, and paid him, under the table, a somewhat low monthly salary—but for him this was a beautiful beginning, an increase on his salary from the zoo. He already understood that it was worth it to him to invest his time and energy into her, because she was sitting on a gold mine. Even to himself he didn't dare think how much she has, not in Egyptian lirah and not in Euros. He also knew that he didn't know everything. He assumed that she has an account in Geneva as well, and there too is a fortune. He knew that she has three apartments on Cairo's high-priced streets, those that Egyptian movie stars live on, and a factory building, which someone from Abu-Dhabi pays high rent in exchange for; and that's without mentioning the key to the women's section, which by itself could be worth an incomprehensible sum; and who knows how much liquid money is located in various other accounts.

Not too long after, Celeste decided that she could trust him, not only because she didn't want to be suspicious like her mother, but she also made some connection among his qualities and came to the overwhelming conclusion that he's loyal. And perhaps he really was loyal. His knowledge of Egyptian history from the time of the Pharaohs, which he didn't keep from her, impressed her. In fact, she was the only soul who agreed to hear him tell tales of Egypt's history again and again. She never learned Hebrew, and she wouldn't need to learn.

They kissed by the cage of the graying black tiger. After the kiss, which was neither long nor short, she took some steps as though to walk away from him, a sign of great embarrassment. Much blood flowed to her cheeks and reddened them considerably.

That afternoon he parked his old blue car next to the villa with the Egyptian palm tree. He entered and behaved in exemplary fashion. Drank an excellent coffee she prepared, and didn't force her into bed. Furthermore, he helped her organize paperwork all evening, and he filed papers into the mother's ring binders, and had no problem deciphering her handwriting. They worked until late at night, and he went from there.

Celeste fell in love with him, and there's no describing the wave of desire she felt whenever they met. Much time passed until her pulse returned to normal. She wanted him to be available for her whenever she wanted—she's a very vulnerable woman and needs an angel to protect her in this difficult world.

The first times were wonderful. She gave in easily, and everything was done under cover of darkness and hastily, like a sinful act. There was good chemistry between then, but he had to work harder than she thought.

But one Sunday Abdallah the veterinarian took his own life, and El-Amwari didn't answer calls because all morning he was busy with funeral arrangements, which he was also forced to pay for with zoo funds; and afterward he went to the funeral with a handful of zoo workers, and he couldn't answer the cell phone during the funeral.

Celeste, who was hurt because he wasn't available by phone, remembered that she needed air. She had never brought a man into her mother's home, and she had many things to think about.

The president who was previously sent to prison was released from prison to his home for medical reasons, in place of the death sentence that it was thought he deserved. Slowly it became clear that the new president wasn't part of the consensus either, and a new coup began. The streets were even more dangerous than before, and Celeste didn't return to the zoo, and didn't answer calls. She didn't respond to any of the messages Fareed left on the answering machine. This angered him a lot, but he waited patiently for the end of the month. Matters requiring his attention would certainly pile up for her.

And indeed, at the end of the month he was called to her home. They sat on the porch for three hours, and she showed him files on top of files that neither he nor she had ever seen before. Most of the documents were in Arabic, and others were in English and German—those from the accounts in Switzerland. He brought a calculator with a paper ribbon, and they began to work and calculate.

He was focused and calculated calculations, and Celeste didn't dare interrupt that seriousness.

"Many people owe you money, do you know that?" he asked her.

From here on out he became her collector, and in a few instances managed to catch up on gaps of a year in payments that he recovered for her, and wherever he arrived with the power of attorney he received from her, actual doors opened up before him, as well as files on the computer, files which for good reasons he copied to his laptop, which also included a window with the zoo's cameras, and this way he could at any moment know what was happening there.

What a gift from the heavens was the bald man standing across from her, Celeste thought, now paying him a very reasonable monthly salary for everything he did, and not under the table: he would stand at her side and listen to her. They would consult and reach conclusions, and everything, of course, was done pleasantly and politely. Finally she has a man, and he even tells her what to do. Says "we" and means her and him.

But not long after their world was shaken again. There was another coup, and the military forces attacked those opposing the new coup, who claimed that their president was elected democratically, and killed fifty-one of their opponents. El-Amwari, who was on the side of those who now took power into their hands, was shocked by the slaughter. Eight days after the army shot live ammunition into the demonstrators opposing the coup, he left his home with his laptop, and disappeared without a trace. Did he find himself in a firefight and was killed and buried anonymously? Celeste went to the police once or twice, but they didn't find him and didn't know what became of him. Also unknown was whether or not every two to three months funds from some remote bank account of hers were withdrawn; there was no knowing, because she herself didn't notice.

Chapter 15
Lucia

THE FULL TRUE story of Lucia lies within the realms of the unmentionable, but one can say some things about her. She bought her leopard-spotted shoes at the store where she got her manicure and pedicure done, on Kings of Israel Street opposite Rabin Square and the Tel Aviv municipality. Upon reaching fifty, after many hardships, of an intensity that was very hard to bear, she moved to an apartment on Chen Boulevard, which was originally a four-bedroom apartment. They turned it into a suite with a bedroom and living room connected to the kitchen. She managed to live there less than two years.

In her final days—even though she was a native of Buenos Aires, and knew Spanish, Portuguese, English, French, Italian, a little Sanskrit, and fluent Hebrew—she received her fate in Arabic of all things, and would often say: *Allahu akbar*, quietly, in her deep, hoarse voice.

Actually, when she was informed of her disease, she was already addicted to muezzins, and especially loved those from remote places in the desert. They helped her to bear the chill of dying alone, and quite quickly she knew how to sing them in all sorts of variations: a muezzin in a godforsaken village in the Sahara, a fanatical muezzin instigating a riot, a moderate muezzin on a calm day inside of whom something bubbles up nevertheless, and more.

When she left her apartment without returning she left all the lights on, and they were on all those days, until her friend the psychiatrist went there, a day after her death, and turned them off.

All the days of her dying all the lights were on, day and night.

On the second day of her hospitalization she called for the hairdresser, so he could cut her hair before the wig and the treatments. The name of the hairdresser was Jackie, and he gave her a short hairstyle, and said that he'd fit her for a wig at no cost. There are no people like you in this country—he repeated this a few times.

Her apartment stood empty for seven months, until the landlady, a Polish woman who also owned a successful café, succeeded in renting it again.

Her dying lasted four days. Two days conscious and two days unconscious, with moans of sorrow at each and every breath. On the first two days, when she was still conscious, the old Russian woman who was lying next to her asked her to leave the curtain between them open and not to push her aside, but Lucia insisted:

"No. Come when I call you."

She controlled matters even after she lost consciousness. Her consciousness would return for moments, and then she asked the Argentinean doctor on call what was happening to her that her consciousness was waning. She spoke with the curly-haired doctor in Spanish, and sometimes she lost consciousness again in the middle of speaking.

Lucia was sensual, and loved food, sex, and perfume. She admired the creators of complex, sophisticated perfumes, perfumes whose scent changed over the hours of the day and according to the seasons, or perfumes suited for different seasons, and after she delved into each subject that interested her, even Sanskrit and its etymological and semantic connections to all sorts of languages that she knew, she turned to research the world of perfumes thoroughly, and bought perfumes by Serge Luten with names like *Fleurs de Citronnier*.

"The scent of perfume has a complex structure like a pyramid, and therefore one must not spray perfume and rub it with the hand, but rather one needs to squirt it on the required places and leave it. If one rubs, one greatly damages the apex of the pyramid, and the perfume becomes superficial and doesn't evolve with the woman over the course of the day," she would warn.

In the message on her answering machine she said in Spanish in her pleasant, low voice: five four four zero nine zero eight; please leave a message after the beep.

At the age of twelve she downed the *Encyclopedia Judaica*, a thing that brought about a clash of continents in her enormous consciousness, and demanded of her action on a similar scale. She then by herself convinced an entire branch of her family to uproot itself from Buenos Aires and immigrate to Israel. In Israel, in Bat-Yam and the Hadasim boarding school, she was disillusioned but didn't despair, and continued to inject motivation into those sitting on the branch that she cut off from the capital of Argentina and brought here in the name of escaping fascism and of the Jewish revival, as she understood it from the *Judaica*.

In Israel she was always in the middle of things—with eyes open she comprehended connections, circumstances, and sent herself to Freudian and Lacanian analysis, and always wanted to know what the truth was, what was really happening all around, and where she was in all of it. First of all, where does she stumble, and then the others—where do they get confused between essence and rubbish. She told her conclusions to too many people in her raised, certain voice, nor did she spare her family members, and gave them, besides *charoset* on Passover, analysis in Spanish as well, especially at the Rosh Hashanah and Passover seder meals. Every once in a while, and sometimes for a long time, she would wander around confused, but focused in an unusual manner, and then her friends knew: Lucia understood "something" about the essence of man, or about the essence of nature and the divine, and now she was immersed in a comprehensive inner examination in regards to every ethos, mythos, and pathos to which she had been exposed.

And eventually, when it appeared that all the alarms were just an exercise by the Home Front Command, the truth descended: breast cancer, which included swelling in the breastbone, where the heart chakra is also located, with metastases in the lungs, about which it was best not to speak.

Therefore she asked the Older Daughter to make her laugh, and in front of Lucia she would imitate her talking on the telephone with her British boyfriend Charles and asking him about the weather there, and would also imitate her reporting on the weather here, saying again and again that a cold day in the middle of the winter in Israel is a summer day from England's perspective, and the two of them would roll with laughter, and Lucia would hold her painful sternum and say: That's wonderful, that's wonderful. Do more imitations for me, please.

And the Older Daughter would imitate whomever she could for her, and would also exaggerate, the main thing being to release the pressure that had accumulated in the base of the sternum.

A month before her death she traveled to England for a workshop on the latest perfumes that had come out on the market, and there she lost sight in her right eye. When she returned to Israel she did a CT and it became clear that the entire brain was full of metastases, as well as the liver and the lungs. But Lucia decided that despite everything she was within the sphere of health, and walked to a café with Parliament cigarettes, which she chain-smoked, and ordered a double espresso, and with her phone took pictures of the people coming and going and of those sitting in the café.

Only on her second day at Ichilov, after Jackie came up to the department to cut her hair short—not too short—did she understand that she was about to die, and she fled in the direction of death when she heard her family members all around speaking with the doctors about the price difference between a private hospice and a hospice sponsored by the state.

Somehow it happened that her brother worked in funerals and burials, while the heavyset psychiatrist friend took over sorting through the personal items, including the clothes and the perfumes and all the cosmetics, which Lucia and the Older Daughter would buy on the Internet in different and strange combinations—the two of them were without a credit card, either an Israeli or international one, and required the cooperation of a third party, with a card, who agreed to assist in the transatlantic business in exchange for smoother access to heaven. Lucia said that he was doing charity for them, and that the universe was likely to reward him for this.

The psychiatrist—whose hair was long and unkempt, and whose face was red, and whose glasses were round, and who knew how to connect with great skill to unruly patients with calm, because after all she had finally gotten tenure—also orchestrated the sorting like that, so no one from among the fifty-nine good friends that Lucia had would take one perfume too many. She cooperated with the brother in imposing authority on the events. Okay, they had to empty the apartment quickly, because her relatives didn't want to pay rent for another month, which was about to start.

There's no doubt about it—her brother and his wife did the bulk of the dirty work. And just before the end, at the instructions of the psychiatrist, the Older Daughter arrived and sprayed onto herself one of the strong perfumes that Lucia brought back from her very last tour in London. When she opened up the drawer all the way she was amazed to discover a stockpile of perfumes still packed in their cardboard boxes, arranged in impeccable order—an inventory for the next ten years – and suddenly an ashtray on the balcony caught her eyes and in it was a cigarette that Lucia had lit and left in the ashtray as usual, until all that was left of it was a thin gray cylinder.

She opened another drawer and there were perfumes in it as well, and next to them make-up for rejuvenating the skin and for creating various brightening effects on various parts of the face, and types of powders, and Chanel lip cream to prevent dryness and give a natural pink touch.

She called Lucia's psychiatrist friend to ask her what to do with all the clothes and perfumes, which unambiguously proved that Lucia didn't think she would die so fast. The psychiatrist friend sobbed into the line and told her not to touch anything. If the Older Daughter wants, take two or three perfumes and samples, and a few shirts, but not that and not that and not that, and please please not that either. But take the black jacket they bought together on sale in London, she can't see it. The psychiatrist friend grew greatly sentimental in those moments, relative to herself and relative to a psychiatrist.

The professor at the Open University, who not long ago turned seventy-five, arrived at the *shivah*. Until the age of seventy he was half the year in Israel and half the year at Rutgers University, in New Jersey. When he turned seventy he decided to live and research only in Israel. All throughout the days of her illness Lucia didn't hear from him, and certainly not throughout the days of her dying, after all he already had another love affair. To the *shivah*—he arrived. Entered through the open door, shook the brother's hands, who treated him with great respect and bowed, and the brother's wife also trembled a bit, after all he's a professor, and had even been awarded many prizes. He sat on the sofa, the cover of which Lucia bought at IKEA—she bought it twice, because the first time the Older Daughter accidentally spilled coffee on it, and it was impossible to remove the stain—consoled the family, even the old father, and hurried back to his business.

Because she died in the winter, it was reasonable that he wore a long black wool coat, wrapped a black wool scarf around his neck, and wore a black beret. After years in Jerusalem, until he retired from there, and more years in Manhattan (when he taught in New Jersey), clearly he wore a black beret.

Wise and generous Lucia contributed significant ideas to the professor's thick books, in exchange for love. As well as priceless advice about how to behave with his problematic son and disturbed wife, the wife he later left, though he beat her first. The ideas are well woven into his books and life, and they can't be extracted with any tweezers.

But one thing is certain: when the professor from the Open University begins an affair, he first verifies that the affair is stable, and only then does he search for a good sale on condoms of superior quality.

When he was residing in Manhattan he entered one of the chain drugstores and bought one hundred and twenty-five superior quality condoms on sale as "one-hundred plus twenty-five free."

Every time the professor and Lucia had sex they did it on a thin, second-hand mattress resting on the floor at her place. Lucia would cover the mattress in premium sheets that she obtained somehow, and prior to his arrival would spray the mattress with perfume appropriate for the season as well.

For five years the professor visited her on that mattress and never thought to buy her a thicker mattress, or even a real bed. The mattress didn't bother him, and maybe he even liked to have sex like that.

Lucia gave him a lot of herself, and one time he gave as well: two sculptures by Kadishman, very heavy, which the Older Daughter kept during the year Lucia spent in England, because she went there to recover, after the affair between them ended.

But before England, there was a time that one of the condoms that the professor bought on sale ripped, and Lucia got pregnant. There were two weeks of joy (on her part), and a lot of deliberations (on his part), because the professor wanted her to abort it, and Lucia wanted the child. The biological clock was ticking. She was already a moment before the age of forty.

During those two weeks the phone rattled many times throughout the day, and every time the answering machine picked-up in Lucia's Spanish voice, the professor pretended that he wasn't up-to-date on the invention of the answering machine, and called into the recording: Hello, hello, hello, hello . . . until the recording time ran out.

And when she answered the phone, he screamed at her to get rid of the fetus. That she's ruining his life, the fetus', and that she has no way to raise him, because he won't support her, the professor, he certainly won't support her, and not the child either.

"What do you have? The two Kadishman sculptures that I gave you?" he said to her once.

Due to the terrifying things he said she miscarried naturally, and the job was finished by a gynecologist, who studied medicine with the psychiatrist at Tel Aviv University in the eighties.

Also arriving at the *shivah* was the Lacanian psychoanalyst, who works with the conservative psychiatrist who knows how to hook people up when they need the tranquility of the hospital where she finally has tenure. Between the psychiatrist, who was Lucia's friend, and the psychoanalyst, who was Lucia's psychoanalyst and a work-friend of the psychiatrist, the boundaries were well-maintained, and at Lucia's funeral they sat next to each other on a rock like two people who had despised each other for some time already.

The psychoanalyst, like the professor, didn't arrive for Lucia's dying either. Apparently because dying is not included in analysis. The analysis ends the moment the person loses consciousness, or irreversibly enters the hospital in leopard-spotted shoes. Moreover, two years before Lucia's death, in the week when she was informed that she's very sick, the psychoanalyst said to the Older Daughter (who was also a patient of hers) when the matter came up in a session that this is the second time that she accompanies a patient to the death. And she shed a tear in one eye, but the other eye only turned red and did not succeed in producing a tear.

Everyone finds for himself a time to come according to the agreed upon boundaries determined by the thesis according to which he operates. For instance, one poet, with a look that God should forbid, as if her eyes were taken from the film *The Shining*—a fabricated woman, who Lucia edited poems for at a café and was her spark plug—didn't come to a thing, not to the funeral and not to the *shivah*, and when the Older Daughter ask her why she kept her distance and didn't come, she responded: "Does it bring back the dead?"

There are eight apartments in the façade of the building where Lucia resided. All of them had the same awning exactly, after an exterior renovation. Again and again the awning of Lucia's apartment filled up with the city's dust and the spit of bats from the rubber plants on Chen Boulevard, and again and again the landlady's handyman cleaned it.

The landlady was very firm in her demands this time. After the quick and mysterious death of the last tenant, she looked for a non-mysterious tenant, under the age of forty, thirty-five preferably, with a nice paystub from a large, well-known company.

When Lucia entered the apartment and paid a year in advance in cash, the stern landlady believed that fortunately an excellent renter had fallen into her hands, for ten years at least. And here she died at the age of fifty-two after only half a year; died while she appeared to be full of strength and beauty, not like others in her condition, who for some time already are rolling down the boulevard in a wheelchair with a Filipino behind them, after a series of harsh therapies.

Only now the landlady had great difficulty finding a tenant to her liking, not to mention those interested in the apartment, immediately upon hearing that the previous tenant died before her time, thought that perhaps it was something in the walls, in the karma, or in the mini-central air system, and fled from there.

The landlady owns several apartments on the finest streets in Tel Aviv, and she also has a penthouse apartment of King David

Street, in which she herself lives. The handyman works for her in all the apartments for twenty years now, and despite this she doesn't pay him a salary, but rather he does it for her piecework.

But finally, after seven months, the landlady found a new tenant, who appeared to her to be an absolutely regular guy, very well dressed, healthy, not fat and not skinny, with a steady job and a solid paycheck. True he didn't pay her in cash like she did, but he paid a year in advance with checks. The landlady signed a contract with him for a year with an option to extend, and the rent was high like she wanted.

But very quickly it was understood that one couldn't know a thing about the new tenant, and there was no doubt that he didn't want anything to be known either. In contrast to the rest of the apartments in front, which preferred western light and Chen Boulevard's green trees, without any shading, this one came along and hung Roman shades, which lowered themselves in a cream color from the top down, and they were always down.

And then everything made sense: the landlady found for herself someone who was already a living-dead from the beginning.

Clever. She was getting the hang of it. There was too much life in Lucia, too much curiosity, too much enthusiasm and creativity—and worst of all, tremendous knowledge, that built new connections for her in her mind, which always left her too lucid, and arose in whoever was listening to her a feeling that he knew nothing about life. She spouted knowledge about all-embracing topics, and shared it with anyone who was willing to be enriched by this knowledge. She even lit up the eyes of the landlady herself.

Apartment number five wouldn't need to switch tenants for a long time now. The apartment had needed someone with stagnated qi, and it got one like that. Now the landlady could sleep in peace. At the most the new tenant would bother her handyman, after all that's what she pays him for, and he's obedient and does whatever she tells him to do.

Orly Castel-Bloom is a leading voice in Hebrew literature today. Her postmodern classic *Dolly City* has been included in UNESCO's Collection of Representative Works, and was nominated in 2007 as one of the ten most important books since the creation of the state of Israel. Castel-Bloom won the Sapir Prize in 2016 for *An Egyptian Novel.*

Todd Hasak-Lowy has published several books for adults, children, and young readers. His translation of Asaf Schurr's *Motti* won the 2013 Risa Domb/Porjes Hebrew-English translation prize. He lives with his wife and two daughters in Evanston, Illinois.

MICHAL AJVAZ, *The Golden Age.*
The Other City.

PIERRE ALBERT-BIROT, *Grabinoulor.*

YUZ ALESHKOVSKY, *Kangaroo.*

FELIPE ALFAU, *Chromos.*
Locos.

JOE AMATO, *Samuel Taylor's Last Night.*

IVAN ÂNGELO, *The Celebration.*
The Tower of Glass.

ANTÓNIO LOBO ANTUNES, *Knowledge of Hell.*
The Splendor of Portugal.

ALAIN ARIAS-MISSON, *Theatre of Incest.*

JOHN ASHBERY & JAMES SCHUYLER, *A Nest of Ninnies.*

ROBERT ASHLEY, *Perfect Lives.*

GABRIELA AVIGUR-ROTEM, *Heatwave and Crazy Birds.*

DJUNA BARNES, *Ladies Almanack.*
Ryder.

JOHN BARTH, *Letters.*
Sabbatical.

DONALD BARTHELME, *The King.*
Paradise.

SVETISLAV BASARA, *Chinese Letter.*

MIQUEL BAUÇÀ, *The Siege in the Room.*

RENÉ BELLETTO, *Dying.*

MAREK BIENCZYK, *Transparency.*

ANDREI BITOV, *Pushkin House.*

ANDREJ BLATNIK, *You Do Understand.*
Law of Desire.

LOUIS PAUL BOON, *Chapel Road.*
My Little War.
Summer in Termuren.

ROGER BOYLAN, *Killoyle.*

IGNÁCIO DE LOYOLA BRANDÃO, *Anonymous Celebrity.*
Zero.

BONNIE BREMSER, *Troia: Mexican Memoirs.*

CHRISTINE BROOKE-ROSE, *Amalgamemnon.*

BRIGID BROPHY, *In Transit.*
The Prancing Novelist.

GERALD L. BRUNS, *Modern Poetry and the Idea of Language.*

GABRIELLE BURTON, *Heartbreak Hotel.*

MICHEL BUTOR, *Degrees.*
Mobile.

G. CABRERA INFANTE, *Infante's Inferno.*
Three Trapped Tigers.

JULIETA CAMPOS, *The Fear of Losing Eurydice.*

ANNE CARSON, *Eros the Bittersweet.*

ORLY CASTEL-BLOOM, *Dolly City.*

LOUIS-FERDINAND CÉLINE, *North.*
Conversations with Professor Y.
London Bridge.

MARIE CHAIX, *The Laurels of Lake Constance.*

HUGO CHARTERIS, *The Tide Is Right.*

ERIC CHEVILLARD, *Demolishing Nisard.*
The Author and Me.

MARC CHOLODENKO, *Mordechai Schamz.*

JOSHUA COHEN, *Witz.*

EMILY HOLMES COLEMAN, *The Shutter of Snow.*

ERIC CHEVILLARD, *The Author and Me.*

ROBERT COOVER, *A Night at the Movies.*

STANLEY CRAWFORD, *Log of the S.S. The Mrs Unguentine.*
Some Instructions to My Wife.

RENÉ CREVEL, *Putting My Foot in It.*

RALPH CUSACK, *Cadenza.*

NICHOLAS DELBANCO, *Sherbrookes.*
The Count of Concord.

NIGEL DENNIS, *Cards of Identity.*

PETER DIMOCK, *A Short Rhetoric for Leaving the Family.*

ARIEL DORFMAN, *Konfidenz.*

COLEMAN DOWELL, *Island People.*
Too Much Flesh and Jabez.

ARKADII DRAGOMOSHCHENKO, *Dust.*

RIKKI DUCORNET, *Phosphor in Dreamland.*
The Complete Butcher's Tales.

RIKKI DUCORNET (cont.), *The Jade Cabinet.*
The Fountains of Neptune.

WILLIAM EASTLAKE, *The Bamboo Bed.*
Castle Keep.
Lyric of the Circle Heart.

JEAN ECHENOZ, *Chopin's Move.*

STANLEY ELKIN, *A Bad Man.*
Criers and Kibitzers, Kibitzers and Criers.
The Dick Gibson Show.
The Franchiser.
The Living End.
Mrs. Ted Bliss.

FRANÇOIS EMMANUEL, *Invitation to a Voyage.*

PAUL EMOND, *The Dance of a Sham.*

SALVADOR ESPRIU, *Ariadne in the Grotesque Labyrinth.*

LESLIE A. FIEDLER, *Love and Death in the American Novel.*

JUAN FILLOY, *Op Oloop.*

ANDY FITCH, *Pop Poetics.*

GUSTAVE FLAUBERT, *Bouvard and Pécuchet.*

KASS FLEISHER, *Talking out of School.*

JON FOSSE, *Aliss at the Fire.*
Melancholy.

FORD MADOX FORD, *The March of Literature.*

MAX FRISCH, *I'm Not Stiller.*
Man in the Holocene.

CARLOS FUENTES, *Christopher Unborn.*
Distant Relations.
Terra Nostra.
Where the Air Is Clear.

TAKEHIKO FUKUNAGA, *Flowers of Grass.*

WILLIAM GADDIS, JR., *The Recognitions.*

JANICE GALLOWAY, *Foreign Parts.*
The Trick Is to Keep Breathing.

WILLIAM H. GASS, *Life Sentences.*
The Tunnel.
The World Within the Word.
Willie Masters' Lonesome Wife.

GÉRARD GAVARRY, *Hoppla! 1 2 3.*

ETIENNE GILSON, *The Arts of the Beautiful.*
Forms and Substances in the Arts.

C. S. GISCOMBE, *Giscome Road.*
Here.

DOUGLAS GLOVER, *Bad News of the Heart.*

WITOLD GOMBROWICZ, *A Kind of Testament.*

PAULO EMÍLIO SALES GOMES, *P's Three Women.*

GEORGI GOSPODINOV, *Natural Novel.*

JUAN GOYTISOLO, *Count Julian.*
Juan the Landless.
Makbara.
Marks of Identity.

HENRY GREEN, *Blindness.*
Concluding.
Doting.
Nothing.

JACK GREEN, *Fire the Bastards!*

JIŘÍ GRUŠA, *The Questionnaire.*

MELA HARTWIG, *Am I a Redundant Human Being?*

JOHN HAWKES, *The Passion Artist.*
Whistlejacket.

ELIZABETH HEIGHWAY, ED., *Contemporary Georgian Fiction.*

AIDAN HIGGINS, *Balcony of Europe.*
Blind Man's Bluff.
Bornholm Night-Ferry.
Langrishe, Go Down.
Scenes from a Receding Past.

KEIZO HINO, *Isle of Dreams.*

KAZUSHI HOSAKA, *Plainsong.*

ALDOUS HUXLEY, *Antic Hay.*
Point Counter Point.
Those Barren Leaves.
Time Must Have a Stop.

NAOYUKI II, *The Shadow of a Blue Cat.*

DRAGO JANČAR, *The Tree with No Name.*

MIKHEIL JAVAKHISHVILI, *Kvachi.*

GERT JONKE, *The Distant Sound.*
Homage to Czerny.
The System of Vienna.

JACQUES JOUET, *Mountain R.*
Savage.
Upstaged.

MIEKO KANAI, *The Word Book.*

YORAM KANIUK, *Life on Sandpaper.*

ZURAB KARUMIDZE, *Dagny.*

JOHN KELLY, *From Out of the City.*

HUGH KENNER, *Flaubert, Joyce and Beckett: The Stoic Comedians.*
Joyce's Voices.

DANILO KIŠ, *The Attic.*
The Lute and the Scars.
Psalm 44.
A Tomb for Boris Davidovich.

ANITA KONKKA, *A Fool's Paradise.*

GEORGE KONRÁD, *The City Builder.*

TADEUSZ KONWICKI, *A Minor Apocalypse.*
The Polish Complex.

ANNA KORDZAIA-SAMADASHVILI, *Me, Margarita.*

MENIS KOUMANDAREAS, *Koula.*

ELAINE KRAF, *The Princess of 72nd Street.*

JIM KRUSOE, *Iceland.*

AYSE KULIN, *Farewell: A Mansion in Occupied Istanbul.*

EMILIO LASCANO TEGUI, *On Elegance While Sleeping.*

ERIC LAURRENT, *Do Not Touch.*

VIOLETTE LEDUC, *La Bâtarde.*

EDOUARD LEVÉ, *Autoportrait.*
Newspaper.
Suicide.
Works.

MARIO LEVI, *Istanbul Was a Fairy Tale.*

DEBORAH LEVY, *Billy and Girl.*

JOSÉ LEZAMA LIMA, *Paradiso.*

ROSA LIKSOM, *Dark Paradise.*

OSMAN LINS, *Avalovara.*
The Queen of the Prisons of Greece.

FLORIAN LIPUŠ, *The Errors of Young Tjaž.*

GORDON LISH, *Peru.*

ALF MACLOCHLAINN, *Out of Focus.*
Past Habitual.
The Corpus in the Library.

RON LOEWINSOHN, *Magnetic Field(s).*

YURI LOTMAN, *Non-Memoirs.*

D. KEITH MANO, *Take Five.*

MINA LOY, *Stories and Essays of Mina Loy.*

MICHELINE AHARONIAN MARCOM, *A Brief History of Yes.*
The Mirror in the Well.

BEN MARCUS, *The Age of Wire and String.*

WALLACE MARKFIELD, *Teitlebaum's Window.*

DAVID MARKSON, *Reader's Block.*
Wittgenstein's Mistress.

CAROLE MASO, *AVA.*

HISAKI MATSUURA, *Triangle.*
LADISLAV MATEJKA & KRYSTYNA POMORSKA, EDS., *Readings in Russian Poetics: Formalist & Structuralist Views.*

HARRY MATHEWS, *Cigarettes.*
The Conversions.
The Human Country.
The Journalist.
My Life in CIA.
Singular Pleasures.
The Sinking of the Odradek.
Stadium.
Tlooth.

HISAKI MATSUURA, *Triangle.*

DONAL MCLAUGHLIN, *beheading the virgin mary, and other stories.*

JOSEPH MCELROY, *Night Soul and Other Stories.*

ABDELWAHAB MEDDEB, *Talismano.*

GERHARD MEIER, *Isle of the Dead.*

HERMAN MELVILLE, *The Confidence-Man.*

AMANDA MICHALOPOULOU, *I'd Like.*

STEVEN MILLHAUSER, *The Barnum Museum.*
In the Penny Arcade.

RALPH J. MILLS, JR., *Essays on Poetry.*

MOMUS, *The Book of Jokes.*

CHRISTINE MONTALBETTI, *The Origin of Man.*
Western.

NICHOLAS MOSLEY, *Accident.*
Assassins.
Catastrophe Practice.
A Garden of Trees.
Hopeful Monsters.
Imago Bird.
Inventing God.
Look at the Dark.
Metamorphosis.
Natalie Natalia.
Serpent.

WARREN MOTTE, *Fables of the Novel: French Fiction since 1990.*
Fiction Now: The French Novel in the 21st Century.
Mirror Gazing.
Oulipo: A Primer of Potential Literature.

GERALD MURNANE, *Barley Patch.*
Inland.

YVES NAVARRE, *Our Share of Time.*
Sweet Tooth.

DOROTHY NELSON, *In Night's City.*
Tar and Feathers.

ESHKOL NEVO, *Homesick.*

WILFRIDO D. NOLLEDO, *But for the Lovers.*

BORIS A. NOVAK, *The Master of Insomnia.*

FLANN O'BRIEN, *At Swim-Two-Birds.*
The Best of Myles.
The Dalkey Archive.
The Hard Life.
The Poor Mouth.
The Third Policeman.

CLAUDE OLLIER, *The Mise-en-Scène.*
Wert and the Life Without End.

PATRIK OUŘEDNÍK, *Europeana.*
The Opportune Moment, 1855.

BORIS PAHOR, *Necropolis.*

FERNANDO DEL PASO, *News from the Empire.*
Palinuro of Mexico.

ROBERT PINGET, *The Inquisitory.*
Mahu or The Material.
Trio.

MANUEL PUIG, *Betrayed by Rita Hayworth.*
The Buenos Aires Affair.
Heartbreak Tango.

RAYMOND QUENEAU, *The Last Days.*
Odile.
Pierrot Mon Ami.
Saint Glinglin.

ANN QUIN, *Berg.*
Passages.
Three.
Tripticks.

ISHMAEL REED, *The Free-Lance Pallbearers.*
The Last Days of Louisiana Red.
Ishmael Reed: The Plays.
Juice!
The Terrible Threes.
The Terrible Twos.
Yellow Back Radio Broke-Down.

JASIA REICHARDT, *15 Journeys Warsaw to London.*

JOÃO UBALDO RIBEIRO, *House of the Fortunate Buddhas.*

JEAN RICARDOU, *Place Names.*

RAINER MARIA RILKE, *The Notebooks of Malte Laurids Brigge.*

JULIÁN RÍOS, *The House of Ulysses.*
Larva: A Midsummer Night's Babel.
Poundemonium.

ALAIN ROBBE-GRILLET, *Project for a Revolution in New York.*
A Sentimental Novel.

AUGUSTO ROA BASTOS, *I the Supreme.*

DANIËL ROBBERECHTS, *Arriving in Avignon.*

JEAN ROLIN, *The Explosion of the Radiator Hose.*

OLIVIER ROLIN, *Hotel Crystal.*

ALIX CLEO ROUBAUD, *Alix's Journal.*

JACQUES ROUBAUD, *The Form of a City Changes Faster, Alas, Than the Human Heart.*
The Great Fire of London.
Hortense in Exile.
Hortense Is Abducted.
Mathematics: The Plurality of Worlds of Lewis.
Some Thing Black.

RAYMOND ROUSSEL, *Impressions of Africa.*

VEDRANA RUDAN, *Night.*

PABLO M. RUIZ, *Four Cold Chapters on the Possibility of Literature.*

GERMAN SADULAEV, *The Maya Pill.*

TOMAŽ ŠALAMUN, *Soy Realidad.*

LYDIE SALVAYRE, *The Company of Ghosts.*
The Lecture.
The Power of Flies.

LUIS RAFAEL SÁNCHEZ, *Macho Camacho's Beat.*

SEVERO SARDUY, *Cobra & Maitreya.*

NATHALIE SARRAUTE, *Do You Hear Them?*
Martereau.
The Planetarium.

STIG SÆTERBAKKEN, *Siamese.*
Self-Control.
Through the Night.

ARNO SCHMIDT, *Collected Novellas.*
Collected Stories.
Nobodaddy's Children.
Two Novels.

ASAF SCHURR, *Motti.*

GAIL SCOTT, *My Paris.*

DAMION SEARLS, *What We Were Doing and Where We Were Going.*

JUNE AKERS SEESE, *Is This What Other Women Feel Too?*

BERNARD SHARE, *Inish.*
Transit.

VIKTOR SHKLOVSKY, *Bowstring.*
Literature and Cinematography.
Theory of Prose.
Third Factory.
Zoo, or Letters Not about Love.

PIERRE SINIAC, *The Collaborators.*

KJERSTI A. SKOMSVOLD, *The Faster I Walk, the Smaller I Am.*

JOSEF ŠKVORECKÝ, *The Engineer of Human Souls.*

GILBERT SORRENTINO, *Aberration of Starlight.*
Blue Pastoral.
Crystal Vision.
Imaginative Qualities of Actual Things.
Mulligan Stew. Red the Fiend.
Steelwork.
Under the Shadow.

MARKO SOSIČ, *Ballerina, Ballerina.*

ANDRZEJ STASIUK, *Dukla.*
Fado.

GERTRUDE STEIN, *The Making of Americans.*
A Novel of Thank You.

LARS SVENDSEN, *A Philosophy of Evil.*

PIOTR SZEWC, *Annihilation.*

GONÇALO M. TAVARES, *A Man: Klaus Klump.*
Jerusalem.
Learning to Pray in the Age of Technique.

LUCIAN DAN TEODOROVICI, *Our Circus Presents . . .*

NIKANOR TERATOLOGEN, *Assisted Living.*

STEFAN THEMERSON, *Hobson's Island.*
The Mystery of the Sardine.
Tom Harris.

TAEKO TOMIOKA, *Building Waves.*

JOHN TOOMEY, *Sleepwalker.*

DUMITRU TSEPENEAG, *Hotel Europa.*
The Necessary Marriage.
Pigeon Post.
Vain Art of the Fugue.

ESTHER TUSQUETS, *Stranded.*

DUBRAVKA UGRESIC, *Lend Me Your Character.*
Thank You for Not Reading.

TOR ULVEN, *Replacement.*

MATI UNT, *Brecht at Night.*
Diary of a Blood Donor.
Things in the Night.

ÁLVARO URIBE & OLIVIA SEARS, EDS., *Best of Contemporary Mexican Fiction.*

ELOY URROZ, *Friction.*
The Obstacles.

LUISA VALENZUELA, *Dark Desires and the Others.*
He Who Searches.

PAUL VERHAEGHEN, *Omega Minor.*

BORIS VIAN, *Heartsnatcher.*

LLORENÇ VILLALONGA, *The Dolls' Room.*

TOOMAS VINT, *An Unending Landscape.*

ORNELA VORPSI, *The Country Where No One Ever Dies.*

AUSTRYN WAINHOUSE, *Hedyphagetica.*

CURTIS WHITE, *America's Magic Mountain.*
The Idea of Home.
Memories of My Father Watching TV.
Requiem.

DIANE WILLIAMS,
Excitability: Selected Stories.
Romancer Erector.

DOUGLAS WOOLF, *Wall to Wall.*
Ya! & John-Juan.

JAY WRIGHT, *Polynomials and Pollen.*
The Presentable Art of Reading Absence.

PHILIP WYLIE, *Generation of Vipers.*

MARGUERITE YOUNG, *Angel in the Forest.*
Miss MacIntosh, My Darling.

REYOUNG, *Unbabbling.*

VLADO ŽABOT, *The Succubus.*

ZORAN ŽIVKOVIĆ , *Hidden Camera.*

LOUIS ZUKOFSKY, *Collected Fiction.*

VITOMIL ZUPAN, *Minuet for Guitar.*

SCOTT ZWIREN, *God Head.*

AND MORE . . .